"…
de

MW01173983

"You can pick up a paperback titled *Death of a Punk*… and then you can start trying to guess what rock bar on the Bowery was the inspiration for the book's main setting…"
        —New York *Daily News*

"Back in the late 1970s when the music world was abuzz, punk rock took over lower Manhattan. First at Max's Kansas City and CBGBs, and then at the Mudd Club and a host of other locations, loud, raucous rock and roll was the name of the game… I recognized many, many people I knew in its pages… a light, fun artifact of its time."
        —Maureen, *GoodReads*

"The generation was blank but the bullets weren't. Hardboiled meets hardcore in John Browner's gripping tale of underground NY noir. The seamy, steamy, squalid side of the 70s music scene comes to life in this pungent plunge into the dark days of CBGBs."
        —Gary Valentine, founding member of Blondie and author of *New York Rocker: My Life in the Blank Generation*

DEATH OF A PUNK

By John P. Browner

Black Gat Books • Eureka California

DEATH OF A PUNK

Published by Black Gat Books
A division of Stark House Press
1315 H Street
Eureka, CA 95501, USA
griffinskye3@sbcglobal.net
www.starkhousepress.com

DEATH OF A PUNK
Originally published in paperback by Pocket Books, New York,
and copyright © 1980 by John Browner.

ISBN: 979-8-88601-069-5

Cover design by Jeff Vorzimmer, ¡caliente!design, Austin, Texas
Cover photo: *Backstage at Max's* © Lisa Jane Persky
Text design by Mark Shepard, shepgraphics.com

First Stark House Press/Black Gat Edition: November 2023

Introduction

By John P. Browner

Death of a Punk seems never to actually die. Forty-four years after its first publication, it has risen again.

I wrote the book because in the '70s, I was a big Raymond Chandler/Dashiell Hammett fan and also a habitué of the nascent Punk Rock scene (although it was mostly known at the time as "New Wave") on the Lower East Side of NYC. I used to hang out at CBGB's in the early days to hear yet-to-be-signed bands like Television, The Ramones, The Talking Heads, Patti Smith, Blondie, and many other less famous. I simply decided to create a kind of fat, bald, failed Philip Marlowe and drop him into the craziness of that scene. Lenny Hornblower was born.

One excellent band I went to see often was The Mumps. The guitarist was my oldest friend. The lead singer was Lance Loud, famed due to his participation in what was perhaps the first reality TV show, *An American Family*. Through him I got to know his mother, Pat Loud, who at the time worked at a literary agency. I mentioned to her that I'd written about forty pages of a trashy detective novel set in the New Wave scene and she told me, to my genuine astonishment, to send it to her at the agency. She read it and said that if I finished it, her agency would represent me. I was flabbergasted because I had been writing it simply to entertain myself; I had NO idea of getting it published or even of TRYING to get it published.

Shortly after I completed it, Ann Patty, a young

editor at Pocket Books, a subsidiary of Simon & Schuster, bought it. And the rest, as they say, is history. Or, put another way, it sank like a stone. There were pockets of high-volume sales, which not-so-coincidentally were located in the only places in the US at the time where New Wave music was popular: NYC of course, LA and San Francisco, but also Cleveland, Boston, Athens, GA, and Seattle. What fan mail I received all came from those places.

Foreign rights were sold to Germany where it went through two printings as *Tod eines Punk* with a truly awful cover; I never received any royalties. A few years ago, the German edition was paid the compliment of being pirated. I sued the guy and won, finally earning some money from Germany! It came out in France entitled *ZZZ*. I sold the film rights three times because would-be producers smelled an album tie-in, and I was paid by one to write a screenplay adaptation, but nothing ever came of it.

In the '90s I was pleased to see that copies were selling online. In 1995 a store in Minneapolis wanted $29.95 for it. I wrote the seller and asked why it was so expensive. He wrote back that he was buying up all the cheap copies he could find because they sold for his price as fast as he could list them. In the next few years, the cheapos pretty much disappeared. Soon the average price had risen to about $50. I couldn't believe it.

I started getting fan mail again because readers were able to find me online. Around 2000 or so, I saw one on abe.com for more than $100. I wrote to the vendor in San Diego and asked him why he was charging such an outlandish sum for it. He responded that every copy he listed sold immediately no matter what the price and that the $100 one had also just sold. He told me he was going to raise the price again if he came across more copies. Prices started to climb into three figures and stayed there for quite a few years. I had to admit it: my book had become collectible! In recent years, prices have descended from the stratosphere to between $50 and $150, which still amazes me.

Because the book is set in the 70's New York City downtown music scene, a time and place now noteworthy, and because some of the peripheral characters seem to be based on real people (although I deny that canard; any resemblance to persons living, dead, or otherwise is purely coincidental and exists wholly in the fevered imaginations of certain wacky readers), it seems to have gained a certain renown. Judging from the fan mail, people seemed to find it funny and entertaining too.

When it came out in 1980, it had no advertising budget. Pocket Books was putting all their chips on the paperback edition of *The World According to Garp*, by John Irving, releasing it with six different covers and a huge promotional budget, and a romance novel by Janet Dailey. The pleasant middle-aged ladies in the publicity department didn't know what to make of *Death of a Punk* (I even had a glowing blurb from Debbie Harry that they didn't use because they hadn't heard of her) and advised me to go to bookstores and buy up copies to extend its shelf life.

They set up a few radio interviews, but I did most of the promoting myself through my connections in the music world. While it got good reviews in hip-but-little-read places like Andy Warhol's *Interview Magazine*, the few reviewers in the mainstream press who wrote about it were a bit nonplussed; the *Denver Post* paired its review of it with an alternate-history novel about World War III by an ex-general. The reviewer segued into the *Death of a Punk* portion thusly: "Going from the globe to the gutter…" which I liked very much. He ended his review by observing that it had "no redeeming social value." which I also liked.

It shares its ISBN with a book titled *Who Killed the Snowman,* which has caused a bit of confusion over the years. The decision makers at Pocket Books had decided to retitle it. When I was told about the change, they also showed me a mockup of the cover. Basically, they wanted to take a book that had to do with the edgy part of the pop music world (which they didn't understand) and change it to the generic part of the drug culture (which they had heard about).

While no expert in marketing, I didn't think it took much brainpower to understand that selling a book as though it's about one thing when it actually isn't, pretty much guaranteed failure. I went into Ann Patty's office, stamped my feet and flailed my arms until she agreed to try to get it changed back to *Death of a Punk*. In the end, we prevailed but not before they'd registered the ISBN as *Who Killed the Snowman?* That's why one can still find mention of *Snowman* in hoary medieval databases.

One side note: The cover with "The Punk." The reason the Punk's left hand is in that goofy position is that in the original painting he was holding a cigarette. The same marketing geniuses who'd come up with *Who Killed the Snowman* decided that potential buyers who didn't smoke or who wanted to quit might subconsciously be deterred from buying the book by the presence of the cigarette. I threw another tantrum but failed to get the cigarette painted back in.

Lenny's ideas and attitudes are those I imagined an urban, working-class guy who came of age in the 1950s might have, influenced more by Sinatra than Presley. Readers have often assumed his attitudes were mine. Not so. To today's readers, some of those attitudes might seem not entirely politically correct. But for that time and place, given Lenny's background, I would argue he was relatively enlightened.

I'm proud that *Death of a Punk* is one of only a handful of works of fiction to come out of the 70's downtown NYC New Wave scene that were published while that scene was still vibrant. I remember at the time being aware that in its own small way the scene was like Paris in the '20s or Berlin in the '30s or San Francisco in the '60s. I thought that one day books 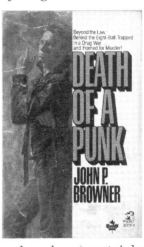 would be written about it (there have been), certainly that some of the music would become classic (and so some of it has), or at least as classic as raw, funny, entertaining music can become. I tried to write a raw, funny, entertaining book with a similar spirit.

I'll let Lenny Hornblower take it from here.

—August 2023

DEATH OF A PUNK
By John P. Browner

Rich or poor, it's nice to have money.
—Traditional

Money will never make you happy and
happy will never make you money.
—Groucho Marx

1

I have an ad that runs in the *Voice* classifieds every week. It says: "ZZZ. Will do private work for a fee. Complete discretion assured. Leonard Hornblower. 212-699-1848." I put it in the Para-Legal Services column because that's where the divorce ads are. That's why the "Z's". It gets put at the bottom of the column underneath "X-Yourself: Divorce—$99 + Tax." Mostly women call me, usually about missing husbands. The guy blows town with his secretary or a topless dancer. The wife gets mad, thinks divorce, checks out the cheapies, sees my ad, and boom: gets a better idea. Or, at least, if she calls, I tell her it's a better idea because I need the money and if I work it right it can add up to a tidy sum. I can't get a decent wage working anywhere else. I can't do anything anyway.

I had a couple of years of college in the late Forties. I did pretty well my freshman year, but I flunked out during the spring semester of my sophomore year because I spent most of my class time composing crossword puzzles and most of my free time drinking. I enlisted in the army and got airmailed to Korea where I machinegunned one Chink, puked for three hours afterward, and bribed a lieutenant to get me transferred to a supply depot in Seoul.

I came back to New York and worked non-union construction for a few years for shit wages. I got sick of that and drove a cab for ten years. In 1960 I married an Italian girl from Brooklyn, Roxanne DiMarino. She wanted kids, I didn't. The argument led to separate bedrooms and two short stays in the hospital for

Roxanne. She left me for points west in 1961 and got some kind of nifty divorce where I didn't have to give her a penny. It surprised me when she got the divorce because she was always yapping about being a good Catholic. Anyway, I haven't heard from Roxanne since.

One day about nine years ago, a fare asked me if I wanted to make a quick fifty bucks. Turned out he was a lawyer who wanted me to follow some guy the next day for three hours. I thought it over for a tenth of a second and said yes.

The mark was a furrier named Schaffner whose store was on Thirty-ninth Street and Seventh. He left the place at 5:30 P.M., took a subway to Sheridan Square, and met some guy in front of Village Cigars. They walked to an abandoned pier-warehouse on Tenth Avenue, went in, came out an hour later, and talked for a few minutes. They kissed goodbye. Schaffner took a bus up Tenth to Thirty-fourth Street, walked to Penn Station, and caught the 8:15 to Babylon.

The next morning I went to the lawyer's office and gave him a report that the widow who lives downstairs from me had typed up. Fifty bucks later I kissed the hack business goodbye.

He threw a few more jobs at me, but they were too few and far between. It occurred to me that I could make more money if I got my own clients, so I stuck the ad in the *Voice*, and it's been easy work for good pay ever since, although the few-and-far-between problem is still with me.

It didn't take long to see how to maximize my profits. A hundred per day plus expenses is nothing for a wife to pay when she finds out that Hubby's in Miami with the dancer. Stretch it out: follow him down there, wait a couple of days—that's what "plus expenses" means—call the little lady, give her Hubby's hotel room number, and let her take it from there. Boom, five hundred bananas and a trip to Florida or Arizona or L.A. Happens four, maybe five times a year.

I can't afford an office; I don't really need one. The telephone in my apartment on West Thirtieth Street is all the equipment I need. I've lived there ever since Roxanne left. The building's kind of shabby, but my apartment is rent-controlled, which means it's cheap, which means I like it. It's a railroad apartment with a living room, kitchen, bedroom, and toilet closet. The bathtub is in the kitchen next to the sink. I sleep on the couch in the living room because I hate making beds and I can't stand unmade ones. The bed gets used when women come over, an event that's become infrequent in the last few years.

I don't have a gun but I always take the black leather sap I stole from a drunk longshoreman with me on my jobs. It's got brass studs on the seam—the very sight of which has three times saved me from irate husbands. I haven't actually hit anyone with it yet.

Every once in a while I get a job tracing runaway kids. They're a pain. I charge one-fifty if it's a kid. Used to be they'd find the worst part of town and flop. Me, a middle-aged, fat, balding square, I'd stick out like a nun in a brothel in those damned East Village tenements. They'd see me and boom, gone. It was all right, though; if it took another day I was one-fifty richer. It was just that it was no fun.

It's changing lately, what with the hippie culture dying out. Now they seem to blow home with a grand at least, rent a room in a nice part of town, buy a load of cocaine and as many downers as they can find. They hit the discos all coked up and then go back to their room and their Quaaludes. I tell the old lady where the kid is. She calls and boom, the kid goes and rents a room somewhere else. I follow and do it again, racking up those one-five-ohs until the kid runs through his wad and toddles home to Scarsdale. Boring, but profitable, which is what counts. It's the only thing that counts. I know.

2

"Hello, hello. Is this Mr. Hornblower?" Probably a nice voice when it's calm.

"Who's calling?"

"I can't give my name, but ..."

"Goodbye."

"No, no." Chalk squeaking on a blackboard. "Okay, okay. My name is Mrs. Perlont."

"Hello, Mrs. Perlont. What's your address?"

"Is this really necessary? I don't see ..."

"Goodbye, Mrs. Perlont."

"No, no. Okay, okay." I felt like I was talking to a duet. "I live at 132 West Eighty-second Street."

"Apartment?"

"5D." She pitched her voice low to get full exasperation out of the "D."

"Thank you, Mrs. Perlont. I like to know who I'm dealing with and where they live before I involve myself in their affairs. You can understand that, right?"

"I could have lied to you."

"Are you home now?"

"Why ... yes."

"As soon as I hang up I'm going to look up your number and call. If you aren't there, I'm going to forget that you phoned."

"Are you through with these games?"

"My ground rules are as follows: I charge anywhere from one to two hundred per day, depending, plus expenses. The ad you read promised complete discretion which is exactly what you'll get. I am not licensed to do my work, so you have to pay me in cash. Two hundred for me to start, and the difference, if any, when you decide I'm finished. I don't carry a gun, so don't expect heroics. I'll call in every day at a time you specify. Questions?"

"No, no. That's fine."

"Okay. Talk to me." I turned on the tape recorder attached to my phone.

She heaved a sigh that said, "I can't believe I'm talking to this jerk," and spoke, "My son …"

"Age?"

"Seventeen."

"Name?"

"Gerald Perlont. His friends call him Blinky. He has a nervous tic under his right eye."

"What's he look like?"

"Um, let's see … about five-eight, uh, about one hundred forty pounds, messy brown hair, green eyes. He wears leather jackets and pants with lots of chains and metal things hanging …"

"Faggot?"

"No, no. He's more like a … a …"

"Biker?"

"Uh-uh. No, he's, well, he calls himself a punk."

"Punk. What d'you mean, a punk? Like a thug, a hood?"

"Oh no, no. It's got something to do with Rock music. He's got this, um … safety pin through his nose. That's supposed to mean something. I don't know what. I think it's a badge or something. I don't know."

She said Blinky had been hanging around a bar where Rock bands play down on the Bowery. It's called AC-DC's. After a while his attitudes and appearance underwent a big change. His marks in school dropped. He was always high on some drug or another and listened to music "that didn't sound like music," according to Mrs. P. He started buying leather clothes and little metal doodads to pin on them. He chopped up his hair so that it stuck out at odd angles and then jammed a safety pin through his nose—for good luck, I suppose. He stole money from his mother to finance his wardrobe. Then about six months ago he bought an electric guitar and an amplifier. His mother—Mr. Perlont is dead—stood it for about four months and then threw the guitar away while Blinky was out.

A fight resulted in Blinky's disappearing for a month. He called every week and told her he was fine and would be home soon. When he did come home, he brought a bad cold and a dose of clap with him. She fed him, nursed him, and got him to go back to school.

Everything was fine until school finished about two weeks ago. Blinky had failed everything. She told him he'd have to go to summer school. He told her where to go and left. She hasn't heard from him since. No calls, no nothing.

"I just can't control him anymore and …"

"Looks that way. What is it you want me to do?"

"If he wants to live on his own, let him. I just want to know where he is, if he's all right, and … if he needs some money."

"You're hiring me to find your son and give him his allowance for one-fifty per day with two hundred up front. You understand that?"

"Yes." She exhaled a sigh. "Yes, I know. I'll invest that much in it just this once to ease my conscience. If he wants to leave forever after what I … well, let him."

A piece of cake. I wished every job was so easy.

"I'll come to your place tomorrow and pick up the advance. I'll be there at eleven A.M., okay?"

"Fine." She sounded relieved.

I hung up, dragged out the phone book, and looked up her number. I dialed. One ring. She picked up the receiver and slammed it down. That was all right. I hadn't asked her to be gracious.

3

I woke up at nine the next morning. Sitting up, I tried to remember what it was I had to do that day. I remembered. I was going to pick up next month's rent from the latest in a long line of tired mothers and wives. The air in the living room was thick and moist. I opened the window, looked out onto Thirtieth Street, and inhaled some July air that was thicker and moister. I took a shower, shaved, and brewed some coffee. I got out a clean white cotton shirt and a pair of brown pants. I put on a tie that had an aerial view of Naples printed on it and slipped on my loafers. Grabbing my snap-brim hat off the hook on the door, I walked down five flights to the street.

The air conditioner on the uptown bus was broken. By Fiftieth Street I needed another shower. By Seventieth I needed a sponge.

Mrs. Perlont's building was just the type of place I've always wanted to live in. It was affluent looking but not rich. It had a marble lobby, a neat but sweaty doorman calling up on the intercom to announce me, twin elevators with old-fashioned wrought-iron gates, and new-fashioned, heat-sensitive, self-service operator's panel. And air conditioning.

The red-carpeted hall was silent as I stepped onto the fifth floor. I walked an ellipse around its length before I found 5-D next to the elevator. Some detective. I knocked.

"Come in, Mr. Hornblower."

She was sitting on a sofa in front of a bay window that looked out onto other bay windows across the street. The room was furnished sparsely. A few paintings, slopped bright acrylic, hung on the walls. A glass tabletop in front of the sofa rested on the backs of two porcelain elephants, one white, one pink. That bothered me. Blessed air conditioning whirred pleasantly in the background.

Mrs. Perlont stood and motioned me to an understuffed, armless chair to the left of the sofa. She was a doll. Slender with blue-jean-wrapped legs: a face that, dotted with green eyes and framed in short, straight, brown hair, had only recently gone from girl to woman and had probably gained in the bargain. Her long peasant blouse dipped obligingly into her cleavage and was tied at the waist, causing attractive folds there and around her breasts. She could have been a model for a tampon commercial.

"Mr. Hornblower, I have an appointment soon." Her tone was more relaxed than it had been the day before on the phone. "Here is the money."

She pointed to an envelope on the table. I picked it up and pocketed it.

"Okay. I won't detain you long. Do you know names and addresses of Blinky's pals?"

"No. Not really. He mentioned something about a girl at that bar who takes money at the door. I don't know her name. We haven't talked much recently."

"I'm sure. When I find him, what do I tell him?"

She looked at my feet for a moment and then into my eyes. I decided I liked green eyes.

"Tell him he's welcome home if he wants, or he can go as far away as he wants." She emphasized "far away." "It's up to him. If he wants some money to start, he can call me and we'll arrange something."

"That's an expensive message."

"I can't figure out any other way to get in touch with him quickly."

"Well, I'll be as quick as I can."

"Thank you."

Her thanks had the sound of "dismissed" to it, so I left. I didn't make a time to call in because I knew I'd easily find the kid that night. This wasn't the kind of job that could be stretched out.

I got on a crosstown bus on Seventy-ninth and switched to a downtown one on Second Avenue. It was just past one when I got to AC-DC's. It was closed. Some winos were hanging around the entrance to a flophouse next to the club. I went to a liquor store around the corner and returned with three quarts of brown-bagged wine.

"Boy, it sure is hot." I opened a bottle and swigged. There were six of them, all black, all drinking vicariously with me.

"Yo, my man." A tall bearded fellow sporting a N.Y. Mets cap stepped toward me. "Don't be hard on us now. You be drinkin' an' not sharin'?"

"Seen Blinky?"

"Say what?"

"Blinky. White boy about my height, wears leather clothes. He's got a safety pin through his nose."

He looked from me to his pals, then back to me.

"Shit, man. I might of seen him. I don't remember."

I handed him the bottle.

"My friends, when they drink, man, it really pushes my remembrance."

I put the other two bottles on the sidewalk. They clustered around and passed them solemnly.

"About our friend Blinky …"

"You say he wears leather clothes."

"Yeah."

"Gotta pin in his nose?" He snorted sarcastically.

"Yeah."

"You talkie' about every l'il suckuh come 'round this place at night, man. They all dress like that, Jack. Them dudes ain't shit. Man, they be actin' all tough an' shit. They pussies, man."

"You never heard of Blinky?"

The runt of the litter was squatting against the wall sucking on a bottle. He spoke in a phlegm-tone voice.

"Yo, this dude, uh … Blinky—he got a funny eye?"

"That's him."

"I seen him 'round here alla time, man. At night."

"Where's he live?"

"Hell, I don't know. You come back tonight. He be here."

Nothing to do but wait. I went back to my apartment and stood in front of the open Frigidaire for about ten minutes. I started to neaten the place up and stopped. I lay on the couch and picked up a book. It was six-thirty when I woke up sweaty, hungry, and with faint memories of dreams of Mrs. Perlont's breasts.

A cold shower and two Swiss cheese sandwiches put me into gear. I picked up a book of Sunday *Times* crossword puzzles from the Thirties and worked on one for about a half-hour. I got dressed and took a cab to AC-DC's.

4

It was just after eight. A different set of bums was there rolling dice on the tiled floor of the flophouse foyer. The white stucco façade of the club was lit by floods tucked under the awning. I pushed open the creaky wooden door and walked in.

It was just like any other brown-black, dingy, dirty rattrap in any city from here to next Tuesday. It was a long, narrow room with a bar along one wall, some tables along the other, and a five-foot-wide wooden walkway splitting it down the middle. Neon beer logos hung from the ceiling. Everything was wood. It looked like someone spent a month at the beach collecting driftwood and then nailed it to the walls, floor, bar, and ceiling with as much discretion as a monkey has on a banana boat.

The walkway ended with the bar, giving way to more tables. Beyond them a plywood stage that looked more like a pygmy's hut rose about three feet from the floor. It was piled high with all those electric music gizmos that give kids such a thrill. A small passage to the left of the stage led to the back where I saw a red exit sign glowing in the darkness. A jukebox blared.

A girl sat behind a table collecting a four-dollar cover from each of the scruffy kids as they filed past. She was slim and pretty but had those tired eyes that said "Whatever it is you want, forget it." You get eyes like that from working in dives like this.

I handed her fourteen dollars.

"Hey," she said, monotone, "you gave me ten too much."

"No. Four to get in, right?"

"Yeah."

"And ten for telling me where I can find Blinky."

She blinked when I said the name. I thought that was funny.

"Well, he's not here. You want to leave a message?"

"No. I'll wait." I walked by her, turned, and spoke to her back. "What bands are playing tonight?"

"The Dogbarfs and Self-Immolation."

"You're kidding."

She swiveled to face me, gave me three seconds of blank stare, and turned back to face the door. She didn't like me. I didn't like her. I hoped Blinky'd show up soon so I could blow this crummy joint.

I walked the length of the place. There were maybe thirty people. No one seemed to be standing or sitting. Everyone leaned. There was nobody dressed in leather or with pins jammed in their faces. I was disappointed. I'd wanted to see that. I went into the passageway that led to the rear. An alcove behind the stage evidently served as a dressing room. Beyond that was a kitchen that doubled as a roach hatchery. A double fire door stood under the exit sign on the back wall. The way this place was set up—narrow exits and large middle, wood everywhere, candles on the tables—a fire on a crowded night and there'd be a lot of barbequed punks. I walked back to the front.

A cigarette machine separated the end of the bar from the foyer where Tired Eyes sat. I sat behind it so I could see the top of her head and whoever came through the door.

By nine the place was starting to crowd up. A few punks had ambled in and clustered along the bench opposite the bar. Leather-clad and chain-wrapped, some wore skinny neckties knotted at the sternum, and others sported studded dog collars around their necks. Almost all had shirts that seemed to be ripped in the same place, as if they had collectively stood in front of a mirror and arranged their tears just so. A few had pins glistening from their cheeks or earlobes. One guy had one through his nose but he was tall and blond. I wanted to ask him if it hurt when he blew his nose, but I was on his turf, and one doesn't like to make the aborigines restless.

The punk girls stood in a group in the aisle, clogging it effectively, making the waitresses perform Buster Keaton acrobatics with their trays of tottering drinks. Their style of dress was more varied than the boys', although the leather, metal, and ripped-clothing motif was still apparent. Tight black jeans and leather jackets surrounded tattered T-shirts covered with illegible red, slashing, felt-tip pen writing that looked like it came from subway car iron-ons. Their painted hussy makeup was just that.

The males of the species seemed to be uniformly skinny and pale. The females were either thunder-thighed or toothpick-limbed. The boys slouched a lot, as if they needed more than their sneakers to support them. The girls' spike heels made them a bit sway-backed as they walked.

Blinky hadn't shown yet. It might be a long wait. I fished out my Marlboros and ordered Scotch.

Three drinks and eight butts later, a guy sat down on the neighboring stool. He looked about twenty-five or so. He had short, dark hair, a clean-shaven face, and the well-oiled smile of a drink too many. He was wearing a white, short-sleeved shirt with a tie skinnier than I'd seen in fifteen years. I don't understand what motivates kids to dress like they do.

"Hi, pal." He handed me his paw. "Come to see the Dogbarfs or Self-Immolation?"

I kept my eye on the door.

"Both," I said, glancing at him. He was gently swaying on his seat, drunk, past the slurring stage into lucidity, which meant he was twenty minutes or one more drink away from incoherence.

"What company are you from?"

"No company. What's it to you?"

"Well"—he propped his cheek in his hand—"adult-type people don't usually come in here unless they're from record companies looking at bands, and I heard from the Dogbarfs' roadie that industry-type guys were coming here, so when I saw you I figured maybe he's an A&R-type guy."

"A what?"

"A&R. I dunno what it stands for. When you read about record company guys and they're not producers or engineers or execs, they always call 'em A&R's."

"What do they do?"

"I dunno. They come here all the time and watch bands. I suppose they're supposed to report back to the company whether the band is good or not. They sit at a table looking all arrogant and stuff ..."

A guy walked in with a goddamn pin through his nose. He was the right height and build.

"... and talk the whole time the band they're supposed to be watching is playing. They either look like retired football players ..."

The newcomer started talking to Tired Eyes, and the back of her head moved like she was talking to him. He looked up quick and stared around nervously from under a thatch of egg-beater hair. The skin under his right eye fluttered.

"... or faggots with stakes up their asses. Bunch of assholes if you ..."

Next month's rent walked past the cigarette

machine.

"Blinky." I said it just loud enough to get through the jukebox noise.

He swiveled his head, focused on me for a moment—his eye twitching like a fish on a hook—and took off toward the back. He had looked at me like he was scared, and not just a little. I didn't like that. It's hard to stop a scared kid and make him listen to you even if all you've got to tell him is to call home for some loot. A chase through a bar full of half-drunk kids wishing it was Berlin in the Thirties was not what I'd had in mind. I didn't feel like doing it. But I did. Mrs. Perlont's tits deserved that much for their money.

He went through the crowd like a snake in a vat of cold cream. I reached the edge of the stage just in time to see the right-hand fire door clank shut.

The gaggle of punkettes had moved their convention into the back passageway by the dressing room. Blinky must have said something to them because they spit curses and saliva at me as I pushed through.

A dark, garbaged alley lay outside the door, blind to the left and opening onto a street to the right. I took two running steps and felt the thud on the back of my head. I remember thinking about Mrs. Perlont as I fell on my side and curled up. I was barely conscious.

Blinky was hovering over me, sweating and mumbling. I tried to talk but all my words came out as groans. I wanted to tell him about the money and his mother and how I didn't mean him any harm. He didn't give me time.

"You tell Nicky from me that I'm through and he'd better not send anyone else after me, or I swear I'll go right to the cops. You got that?" he said through clenched teeth as he kicked me in the stomach. "You got that?" I guess he inherited the twice-told trait

from his mother. He kicked my stomach again and
knocked out my wind. He kicked my forehead and
put out my lights.

5

I became aware of a distant throbbing. At each pulse
the darkness became a shade lighter. As my eyes
opened, a dull ache seemed to begin in my back. I lay
curled, and focused on a bent beer can. The ache moved
up my spine into my head and found a home just in
back of my eyeballs. It throbbed, but with a different
rhythm from what I had first felt. The ground beneath
me seemed to vibrate. I shook my head and inhaled.
The ground was vibrating. I could feel it and hear it.
My body managed to remember a sitting position. I
knew where I was. I was in a filthy alley on skid row
with a battered head. I was lucky the kid had worn
sneakers. He must have hit me with a piece of rotten
wood, or he wouldn't have had to kick me to put me
out. Small blessings. The throb in my head was still
competing with the weird noise that was making the
ground shake. It was coming from AC-DC's. I
wondered if it was the Dogbarfs or Self-Immolation.
    Twelve-fifteen. I'd been out for nearly two hours. At
least he hadn't taken my watch. I'd earned my pay.
The kid was in some kind of trouble and the first
person he'd turn to if he needed help would be his
mother. I decided to call her the next morning, give
her my honest opinion of her twitchy son, and
terminate our little arrangement.
    I got up slowly, letting the blood find its way to my
feet in its own good time. I felt my head. It was well
lumped but dry. More small blessings. My stomach

muscles felt like a training ground for Sherman tanks. My clothes were damp with sweat and had souvenirs from my repose in the muck hanging from them like Christmas tree ornaments. I dusted them off. A piece of string dangled from the button on my right rear pocket. As I brushed it away I felt the unfamiliar feeling of my hand on my ass. Unfamiliar because my right rear pocket is where I keep my wallet and my wallet was where I had placed next month's rent.

I don't mind some scared kid laying lumber on my head. For all he knew, I was going to do the same to him. I'd have a headache for a couple of days, but at least it would have been a two-hundred-dollar headache. Nobody but nobody—I don't care who— takes my money. Especially money that I took a beating for. Blinky was going to pay two hundred dollars and one beating's worth, maybe more.

Tired Eyes was my only connection. I could go back into the club and pressure her, or I could wait until she finished work and try to get something out of her in a more secluded setting. The alley would do fine.

The liquor store I had been to earlier was just closing up. A couple of loose bills I had in my pocket and some change bought me a half-pint of Scotch to keep me company while I waited for Tired Eyes to show.

My bruised face and filthy clothes made me anonymous in that part of town. I ambled over to the dice-rollers at the flophouse, sat on a fire hydrant, and thought about the apartment I would get when I finally found a way to put some real money together. I've thought about it a lot. I do quite a bit of waiting around in my line, and dreaming about my place always passes the time well. Sometimes I furnish the living room or play pool in the second bedroom that I

converted into a billiard room. A woman is always
there, but she never has a face, just a slim body in
tight slacks and a button-down shirt. Sometimes after
I play a few racks I sit down with her on the couch,
turn on the color TV, and slowly unbutton her shirt.

It was two-thirty when she came out. A band's noise
spilled onto the sidewalk with her. She leaned against
the stucco wall and rubbed her eyes. I moved into the
shadow in a doorway and watched. She took a couple
of steps in my direction and stopped, lips pursed, eyes
staring at the sidewalk. She seemed undecided about
where to go. I liked that. Maybe she'd lead me to
someplace interesting.

Turning on a dime, she took off downtown at a near
trot. I gave her one block's grace, polished off the
Scotch, and followed. She turned east on Delancey,
slowed down, walked two more blocks, and stopped in
the middle of the next in front of a gray, four-story loft
building.

Still a block away, I squatted against a storefront
and tilted my head down. Bum disguises are easy
because anyone can be one.

The area was empty and quiet. A gypsy cab slowed,
tooted its horn inquiringly at her, and went by. A siren
flared and ebbed in the distance.

She stepped into the street and stared at the upper
floors of the building. I couldn't see if any lights were
on from the angle I had, but I assumed from her slow
gait to the door that there weren't. Her hand reached
into the doorway. A buzzer that sounded more like a
fire alarm rang loud in the city night. She stepped
back and waited. No answer. Her shoes clacked on
the pavement as she walked toward and by me.

She walked another block and turned back uptown.
It looked like I'd have to apply some pressure after

all. It wouldn't be hard to get Blinky's address from her. My penknife at her throat would accomplish that much. I'd hate myself in the morning but money is money, and Blinky had mine.

A brown van sped by going east. It braked hard, made a "U," and stopped. Two guys in leather jackets got out and went up to the door that wouldn't open for Tired Eyes. That interested me. One went to the back of the van and opened the rear. The other jangled some keys around and opened the door to the building. He propped it with a brick and joined his friend at the van. They pulled out a large black box and carried it into the building. I wouldn't have thought anything of it if not for the fact that the word "Dogbarfs" was stenciled in large white block letters on the box.

I should have figured that some members of the band lived there, and that these clowns were just bringing back some of the equipment. I should have figured that Tired Eyes was friends with them and had come to visit but they weren't home. I should have figured that but I'm just a dumb, lonely man who doesn't think things through. Maybe that's why I live in a five-floor walkup and follow pretty girls around the Lower East Side at three in the morning.

I ran into the building and stepped into the shadow underneath the stairway. I poked my head out and looked up into the narrow shaft formed by the opposing banisters. Two right hands grasped the railing on the top floor. A door opened and sounds of movement came down.

The one-two rhythm of people going downstairs as fast as they can sounded. They reached bottom.

"Hey Jook, wait a sec," a high-pitched voice whined.

"Whaddya want?" Hoarse, toneless. "We gotta get this shit up fast, man."

"Nicky's not gonna like it. You know he told us not to mop anything from AC's. He don't want no connection between the club and the stuff. You know that."

"Yeah, well, we didn't take it from AC's, did we? Those jerks parked their truck around the corner, didn't they? And we didn't take it all, right? Just two heads and a cabinet. That's a fuckin' Jersey band, man. They'll be in Paramus and it'll be tomorrow before they see anything's gone. And we'll get our cut just like always and Nicky won't know the difference, will he?"

"If he finds out he'll hand us our heads on a platter."

"Well he ain't gonna find out, and if he does find out, it means that you told him, and if you tell him I'll hand you your fuckin' head on a platter. You got that?"

Shoes slid on the tile floor followed by a whump of a back against the wall.

"Okay, man"—more whine—"lighten up. I ain't gonna tell Nicky. I just know if Blinky was around we wouldn't of done it because you can't make him do stuff like you make me."

"Well Blinky ain't around, and that's his problem, ain't it? 'Cause when Nicky gets ahold of him, his ass won't be worth shit in a sewer."

"You're damn right about that."

"Hey, I'm right about everything. You remember that we'll have no problems, right? Now let's bring those amps up and get the fuck out of here."

They stepped out and returned quickly with two rectangular gizmos. They climbed the three flights, stayed there for less than a minute, and ran down the stairs and out the door.

I waited for the sound of the van driving off. There were moths burning themselves on lightbulbs on each floor. The top landing was a four-by-eight rectangle with a metal ladder crawling up the wall to a skylight. The lock cylinder on the wooden door was surrounded by a bolted steel plate and a steel guard protected the catch. I pushed it just above the lock. The metal rod of a police lock rattled in its floor socket. There was an eighth-inch space at the door's base.

A locksmith once told me that the weakness of police locks is that they can be used two ways. The first, by a simple adjustment in the gear that pushes the rod in and out of lock, is that the door can only be locked from the outside; you can't lock yourself in. The opposite adjustment allows you to push the bar into place manually should you want to. The problem with that is what can be locked from the inside can be unlocked from the inside.

I went downstairs and stuck a cigarette filter into the lock on the front door. A wire-mesh trash basket stood next to a burned-out lamppost on the corner to my right. There were two more across the street, and I could see another a block away. The first yielded a piece of wood that was too short and probably not strong enough anyway. The second, nothing. My night for garbage. Lying on top of the fifth one like an offering from the god of trash was a wire clothes hanger.

Breaking and entering is not my line at all. But this job was beginning to look bigger than two hundred dollars. I had the feeling that whatever was inside that loft was worth a lot to someone, and what's worth a lot to someone can be made to be worth something to someone else. Like me. But first I had to know what that something was.

The hanger, unwound and straightened except for the hook, was a yard and change long. Judging by the height of the lock, the rod was about four and a half feet. I algebraed it around in my mind and decided the wire might be long enough or it might not be. So much for algebra.

I slid the wire under the door and wiggled it until I felt it slap against the rod. I maneuvered it, trying to get the hook around the rod. It was easy. Now there were two problems. If the lock was set to not open from the inside I was sunk before I began. If it was set to open that way, the wire hook might straighten out from the pressure of pulling it before the rod moved.

I squeezed into the corner to make the angle as obtuse as possible. I started to pull slowly and steadily, exerting the least possible pressure on the wire. The rod felt about as ready to move as a fat lady in a sauna. The hook was straightening out under the pressure. I gave it one hard jerk and the hook came loose, but not before the rod had moved in its housing.

I stood up and gave the door a hard push. It opened quietly into blackness. I felt pretty proud of myself and made a mental note to never get a police lock. They probably only keep out police.

6

The large box I had seen carried in was sitting in the spill of light from the hall. I closed and locked the door and sat on the box to wait for my eyes to accustom themselves to the darkness. Soft light shone in from the street making hazy rectangles on the ceiling. Occasional creaks and rattles broke the silence.

The room gradually defined itself in shades of gray. Three large windows faced Delancey Street. A length of wall twenty-five or thirty feet long opposed them. The doorway I had entered was near one end of the wall. All along the rest of it black hulks climbed to different heights, some nearly to the level of the fifteen-foot ceiling. On the floor were more black piles in five rows of three.

I walked to the nearest and felt it: a canvas tarp with hard corners protruding from underneath. I pulled up the tarp and lit a match. The bottom of the pile was made up of large speaker cabinets arranged in a circle. On top of those were smaller cabinets that had dials and gadgets in a row across their tops. Long flat cases were sitting on the top tied together in two bundles with rubber straps. I stood on one of the speakers, undid the straps of the bundle nearest me, clicked open the three stays of the top case, and lifted the cover. A gleaming black electric guitar with a long beige neck sat in a bed of red felt. The words "Fender Stratocaster" were printed on the end of the neck. I closed it and retied the straps. Every one of the boxes had the word "Fender" diagonally emblazoned in metal lettering on them like logos on cars.

I walked over to a smaller pile and lifted its tarp. The stuff was arranged in the same way, only most of the cabinets were smaller and there were no guitar cases. Everything was labeled "Ampeg."

One of the piles against the wall wasn't covered. Twenty or more guitar cases of varying shapes and sizes stood piled. Next to it was another heap of flat cases that were thicker and not as long. I fumbled with the catches of the top one. A section of the length of the cover came off easily, revealing the black and white teeth of a keyboard. I compulsively pressed the plastic middle "C." No sound. I forgot that you had to plug all these things into sockets to play them. I wondered how Punks pay their electric bills.

I went back to my box and sat down to think. Someone had a thriving business going in electric music equipment. Someone named Nicky. But how did he sell all that crap? You don't lug a three-by-four cabinet to an alley near Fourteenth and Third and wait for a punctured punk to walk by and buy it.

I noticed a door on the other side of the loft catty-corner to the end window. I made my way to it through the piles and pushed it open. I closed the door and lit a match. The chain to an overhead light dangled in front of my face. There were no windows, so I turned it on. It was a narrow room with a walk space bounded on one side by shelves of cardboard boxes and by a workbench on the other. The boxes had words and numbers magic-markered on them. Each contained a different kind of wire that had different jacks and adaptors attached. On the floor underneath the shelves was a long footlocker. I lifted the cover and looked at microphones, lots of microphones. Some were thin and streamlined, others fat with golf ball silver heads. The workbench had hand tools strewn about on it, a couple of power drills, an electric sander, and what looked to be some kind of engraving tool. Underneath were boxes containing small metal plates, some not more than an inch long, others two- or three-square inches. I picked up one of the larger ones. It had a hole in each corner and the word "Fender" etched along one side in the same script I had seen outside.

A louvered door, hinged in the middle, stood at the opposite end of the room. One of the slats at about eye level had fallen out, leaving a small space. I pushed the door to the side. Shiny metal rods were tied together in bundles. Metal discs more than a foot in diameter were stacked in three piles along the back wall of the closet. Microphone stands.

The sound of the outer door opening sent my stomach to my feet. I switched off the light, wedged myself into the closet, and pushed the louvered door shut. Voices and steps came closer. I tried to think of some clever line to say if they caught me. Something about queers and closets came to mind, but I knew I'd never pull it off. I decided to pretend that I was unconscious. Typical—I always want to go to sleep in an emergency.

The door opened and the light went on. I could see about half the width of the room through the broken slat. Black, uncombed hair bobbed in and out of my picture. It started to talk.

"Nicky, I swear it was Jook's idea. He made me do it, man. I told him not to, I swear." It was the whiner again, only now he was practically crying.

"I want you to understand something." I knew the voice but I couldn't glue a face to it. "You are a shithead. Jook is a shithead. What are you?" He didn't sound angry. He sounded like a father telling his son not to play with Daddy's razor.

"Come on, Nicky."

"I said, 'What are you, Stu?'" Slapping. Three times, fast. The black hair jumped with each whack.

"A shithead." Whispered.

"And what is Jook?"

"A fuckin' shithead." Much more conviction.

"Me and Artie have an agreement. He doesn't care that I rip off the bands that play his place as long as I don't do it around his place. I pay him money not to care. That's overhead-type money, y'know. I don't make money on that money. It's gone. And then you two decide you're gonna be cute. You know what Artie's gonna do if he finds out? I'll tell you. He's gonna want more overhead-type money to keep on not caring. You're lucky Walt's out cruising on Christopher Street, because if he was here, I'd give him one of those goosenecks from the closet and tell him to enjoy himself. He keeps telling me that the boys at the S&M bars are no fun anymore. They like it. He wants to beat boys bloody that don't like it. And baby, you qualify."

"Nicky, man, I'll never do it again." The words spilled out so fast I could barely understand them. "I swear. Never. It was Jook. I swear. He said he'd total me if I didn't. He said you'd never find out and we'd get our cut same as always, and if I told, he'd beat me up. He said it. He did. I swear."

"Yeah, well, I'll deal with Jookie-boy. You just stay in line. If it happens again, you'll see Walt. Believe me, you'll see Walt."

"It won't happen again, Nicky. I sw—"

"Shut up. Did you see Blinky tonight?"

"No. I haven't seen him for three days."

"Well, I saw him at AC's. He took off out the back and some guy ran after him before I could do anything."

"Who?"

"I'm not sure. I don't think he was a cop. He was real straight-looking, chubby, middle-aged. Blinky must have conked him, because he was lying in the alley when I got out there. I searched him. Didn't even have a wallet."

"I bet Blinky lifted it."

"Yeah. That's what I think. I'm also thinking Blinky tried to unload some of the stash on him and they argued over price or something, so Blinky conked and fleeced him."

"I dunno. Doesn't sound like Blinky."

"Yeah, I know. But Blinky's scared. He's got three pounds of blow that he stole from Birmingham. He knows that Birmingham wants his ass, which means that I want his ass, which means that Walt wants his ass. Blinky wants to sell it fast and leave town fast. He's scared shitless, so he's likely to do anything."

"I guess you're right."

"I got something for you to do. You're about the only person that knows both Blinky and me that Blinky won't be scared of. I want you to get word to him that I want to buy the coke back at, say, ten grand a pound, and that I guarantee he won't get hurt."

"How do I find Blinky if you can't?"

"You don't have to find Blinky. Find Dora. Tell her to tell him and then set up a meet through her."

"I think Blinky ain't gonna fall for it, Nick."

"Stu, do me a favor. Don't think. Just do what I tell you."

"Okay. I think she's working the door again tonight. I'll talk to her at AC's."

"Good. Now get out of here. I'll lock up."

"Okay. Bye, Nicky."

The door opened and closed. Blood pounded against the inside of my forehead where Blinky had kicked me. I had been sucking air in short breaths as quietly as I could and I was beginning to feel dizzy. Scratching noises at floor level brought me around. Three sharp taps of metal on metal sounded, followed by a slight creak. Whispering. He was counting something. Another creak, another loud tap, the light went off and the door closed. I waited for the sound of the police lock cranking into place and counted slowly to a hundred before pushing the door open. I turned on the light and saw a hammer and chisel on the workbench that hadn't been there before. I knelt and looked at the floorboards. The board parallel to the workbench had little chip marks along one side of its length. I got the hammer and chisel and pried it up. Balls of aluminum foil reflected the overhead light. There were six of them, each about four inches in diameter. I picked one up, unwrapped the foil, and looked at a clear plastic sack of white powder.

I took a shoebox marked "Y-cords" from the lowest shelf, dumped its contents into another box, and put the six balls into it. I toyed with the idea of leaving a note in the hole and signing it "Blinky," but there was no need to be cute. This was a clean steal.

It took an hour to walk home. The drunks along the Bowery were calmly sleeping in doorways or against chicken-wire fences. The air was still and warm. The sun was an hour away from rising. I tried to think about what I had gotten myself into, but my thoughts kept drifting. I thought about calling the police and telling them about the loft and the cocaine, if it was coke. I saw myself as the star witness at the trial. My picture would be in the bottom lefthand corner of the front page of the *Post*. It would show me entering the courtroom with a heavy police escort protecting me. Then I thought about what my life would be worth if I even lived to be the star witness. This wasn't nickel-and-dime missing husbands. This was money: six pounds of cocaine, an organized hijacking ring, and God knows what else. Somebody was going to be very mad at me.

On the other hand, nobody knew I had the stuff. Nobody knew who I was except Mrs. Perlont. I'd tell her I couldn't find her creepy kid and that I couldn't, in good conscience, take any more of her money, and that would be that. I'd wait a few months, figure out some way to sell the drugs, and find a nice apartment with a pool table on the Upper East Side.

It was a pleasant thought for about ten blocks. I started thinking about Blinky and what a dumb kid he was for getting into the stupid jam he was in. The two hundred he stole from me wouldn't help much in his situation. I looked at the clock over the library at Sixth Avenue and Tenth. I checked my watch. It was slow. I started to adjust it, glad again that Blinky hadn't taken it. I stopped and shut my eyes tight. I conjured up a mental image of Blinky, opened my eyes, and gave him my best right cross to the jaw. The force of the swing jarred the shoebox out from under my left arm and sent balls of cocaine rolling on the sidewalk. I gathered them up, swearing. My wallet had my driver's license in it, my address, everything. If he heard the coke was gone, which he would if he lived long enough, he'd know who might have it, where he lived, even what his goddamn middle name was. Of course, he might not put two and two together. Why should he? I couldn't take the chance. I had to find that punk before Nicky did.

7

It was five-thirty when I got home. I wrapped the shoebox in brown paper and addressed it to myself care of General Delivery, Thirty-fourth Street Post Office. My eyes were stinging from exhaustion. I set my alarm for nine-thirty, undressed and went to sleep on the couch.

I dreamed of Mrs. Perlont again. I was sitting in an uncomfortable chair watching her undress. Her hair was cut short like one of the punkettes I had seen at AC-DC's. She took off a dress and a blouse and was naked for a moment. Then she started to take off a short skirt and a T-shirt. She stood in front of me in a white bra and panties and climbed on the back of one of the porcelain elephants. When she got her balance, she was dressed in a black leather bodysuit. A safety pin was stuck through her right nostril and blood dripped down into her mouth. Her tongue made clicking sounds as it lapped the blood and beckoned me at the same time. A zipper ran diagonally from her right shoulder all the way down to her left foot. I reached for it and slowly began to pull. Her breasts appeared. They were small and firm and white. I kissed each nipple once in anticipation of slow, tender lovemaking.

Something frightened me. I pulled the zipper as hard as I could. It made a loud buzzing noise on its way down her leg. I opened my eyes and turned off the alarm.

I stood up and started to inhale slow, deep breaths. Some phlegm came up. I coughed it into the kitchen sink. Every cell in my body was screaming for more sleep. I went into the bathroom and took a fifteen-minute hot shower and a five-minute cold one. My stomach had a red welt on it the size of a small pizza.

I figured it would hurt if I laughed, but there wasn't much chance of that. I shaved and examined the bruise on my forehead. It was impressive, but not very severe. I decided to give Blinky a bruise that wouldn't show but would hurt like hell.

It was going to be another hot day. The sunlight coming in the window had a steamy, still quality that made me think of bubbling tar. I fished out some money from the metal box under the couch, got dressed, tucked my package under my arm and left.

The man at the post office weighed the parcel: six

pounds, twelve ounces. Two dollars and thirty cents later, I was on my way to the coffee shop on Thirty-second Street. I ate eggs and potatoes for sixty-nine cents, the "Breakfast Special." I don't usually have more than coffee in the morning, but I needed something to do with my mouth while I thought over my next move.

I decided to make a list of facts on my napkin while I sipped coffee and released silent, egg-flavored burps.

1. Blinky stole three pounds of cocaine from someone named Birmingham.

2. Tired Eyes' name is Dora.

3. Stu, Nicky's boy, is going to try to set up Blinky tonight through Dora.

4. Blinky has my wallet.

5. Blinky thinks I'm Nicky's man, hired to get him.

6. Nicky's voice is familiar.

7. Nicky runs a hijacking ring.

8. Nicky's strongman is a faggot named Walt.

9. I stole six pounds of what is probably cocaine, maybe heroin, from Nicky.

I put the list aside for a few minutes while I finished the coffee. I picked it up and reread it. I wrote it again in a different order and put it aside again. I read it one cup of coffee later. The only thing that jumped out at me was "Blinky has my wallet." Take that out and none of the others mattered to me.

I paid my check. The Greek waiter sneered at my tip. He was lucky. I don't usually leave one.

It was just past noon when I called Mrs. Perlont from my apartment.

"Hello, Mrs. Perlont?"

"Yes?"

"Hornblower." I tried to sound matter-of-fact. "I looked for Blinky last night and …"

"Oh, Mr. Hornblower, I'm glad you called." My dream flashed through my mind. "He came home last night, so I guess it was all for nothing."

"What?"

"He came home."

"Is he there now?" My intended nonchalance was as subtle as a bulldozer.

"No, no. He just went out. Is something wrong?"

"Oh, no. But I would like to speak to him. When do you think he'll come back?"

"I don't know. I was so relieved he was home I didn't want to annoy him with questions like that."

"Um, listen, I'd like to speak with him. Can I come and wait for him to get back?"

"About what?"

"I heard something last night that he should know about."

"I'll tell him. What was it?"

"No. I'd rather speak to him myself."

"Well, if you insist. I'll have him call you."

"No." I nearly shouted it. "It's something I have to talk to him about in person. It's important."

"Well, I suppose it will be all right. When will you come?"

"I'll be there in a half-hour."

"Okay." She said it thoughtfully. "Okay, I'll tell the doorman to let you in."

"Thank you very much."

"Goodbye."

"Bye."

I got on the same goddamn broken-down bus as the day before. A newspaper was on the seat next to me. I picked it up and got ink all over my sweaty hands which I absentmindedly wiped on my gray slacks. I hate being dirty.

The doorman eyed my bruise as I passed.

"I walked into a door, man."

He stared blankly.

"Get it?"

He shook his head and walked away. My jokes are few and far between. He should have appreciated it.

"Hello, Mr. Hornblower."

I looked straight into her green eyes as she answered my knock. My stomach knotted.

"Thanks for letting me come up. I don't want to inconvenience you, but it's important that I talk to Blinky."

I walked in. Coffee for two was set out on the glass table. The porcelain elephants smiled at me as I sat on the sofa.

"Make yourself comfortable." She walked into the kitchen. My eyes locked on her denim-clad buttocks. "I just have to finish putting away some dishes."

I leaned back and sighed. It was comfortable. I pretended it was mine—a nice air-conditioned apartment, wifey sounds coming from the kitchen; I even liked the elephants. I gave the white one's ass a little kick. The dull, solid note that sounded mingled with the sounds of clinking dishes coming from the kitchen.

A narrow corridor faced me on the other side of the room. At its end was a peach-colored, tiled bathroom whose small window let in the midday sun. Bras and panties hung from the shower curtain rod. I liked that, too.

Two doorknobs extended into the hall about halfway down, bedrooms, probably. I went to see if one was big enough for a pool table.

The lefthand one was hers. Beige diaphanous curtains hung over a drawn venetian blind. A dark brown bureau with a marble top and brass fittings on the drawers stood solidly against one wall under a diamond-shaped mirror. The bed was large and unmade. It had pink-and-white-striped sheets. A nothing nightie lay crumpled on the floor. I could see her getting out of bed—maybe she had stretched a bit and rubbed her eyes—and pushing the straps of her nightie off her shoulders, letting it slide down her body onto the floor. I snapped my fingers to erase the image. A copy of *Looking for Mr. Goodbar* lay open on the lamp table next to the bed.

The posters of Thalidomide rock stars in varying stages of frenzied agony on the door across the hall left no doubt that it was Blinky's room. I walked in. Posters and album covers adorned the walls. Magazines, Nazi doodads, and clothes covered nearly every inch of the wall-to-wall carpet. Blinky liked to live close to the ground. Even his mattress was on the floor. There wasn't any furniture. A closet opposite the door was filled with black leather clothes, all neatly hung and arranged—order in the midst of chaos.

A small address book lay among the sheets on the bed. I put it into my pocket. After all, my address book was in my wallet. It was a fair exchange.

"Mr. Hornblower?" She was still in the kitchen.

"I was just going to the bathroom."

"It's at the end of the hall."

"Right. I see it."

I walked in, peed, then rinsed my face. Something red in the flowered, plastic trashcan caught my eye— bloody tissues, a lot of them. I walked back to the living room.

"Your coffee's getting cold, Mr. Hornblower."

"My friends call me Lenny. What do your friends call you?"

"Lisa."

"The coffee's good, Lisa."

"You haven't tasted it yet."

"Yeah, well." I sipped. "I was right. It is good. That's one of the first things you learn when you become a detective—how to tell good coffee from bad without tasting it."

She laughed a nice laugh. "That's not funny, Lenny."

"I know. You should have seen the doorman crack up at my last joke."

"José laughed?" Her eyes grew wider as she giggled. "I've never even seen him smile."

"Actually, he looked at me like I was a midget leper."

"That's more like it." She focused on my forehead. "What happened?"

"Nothing. I fell down."

"You should be more careful."

"I plan to be."

"Would you like a Danish or something with your coffee?"

"Sure. A Danish would be fine."

The phone on the small table by the door rang as she got up.

"Hello," she said, facing me, smiling, her head tilted to the side. "Yes, I … well, if you can … no." She swiveled on one foot and showed me her back. I preferred looking at her front, but her back would do.

"I can't talk now…. Okay, okay…. Just do it quickly, okay? Quickly…. Right. Bye-bye."

She hung up and exhaled noisily. I had the feeling our little party was over. She turned, put one hand on a hip, and looked at me like I was some curiosity in a junk store.

"Bad news?" I asked.

"No, no." She said it absently. I wanted to hold her

and plant soft kisses on her neck. I sipped some coffee.

"What was I in the middle of doing? Oh, right, your Danish."

She walked into the kitchen. I was tired. I wanted to take a nap in her bed—with her in it.

The door opened. Blinky walked in.

"Hey, Lisa." He turned to close the door. "I …"

I grabbed his shoulders, spun him around, and gave him my best right cross to the temple. He fell back against the door. His knees buckled as he clutched his forehead and leaned forward from the waist.

I half-carried him to the chair by the sofa.

"That's so you don't run this time, jerk."

"What the hell are you doing?" Lisa shrieked, stepping back into the room.

"I had to put Junior in a receptive state of mind."

"Get the hell out of here *now*. Now—before I call the police."

Blinky tried to stand. I pushed him back into the chair.

"To tell you the truth, I don't think you'll call the police."

She walked across the room toward the phone.

"If you call the police and they come, I'll have to tell them about the bloody tissues in the bathroom."

"What?"

"Yeah. You see, somebody had a bloody nose. Some people get bloody noses from being socked, or they get them for no reason at all. But some people get them from snorting cocaine. Right, Blinky, baby?"

"Fuck you." His eye was twitching steadily.

"The police will analyze the blood and find traces of coke. Then we'll all take blood tests and one of us will get busted. And I'm glad to say it won't be me. Right, Blink?"

"Eat shit."

"Now look, look." She wiped her hands on an imaginary apron. "I hired you to find him. Then I told you it wasn't necessary. Why don't you just go and leave us alone?"

Blinky looked at her like he'd just seen a mushroom cloud above the skyline.

"You did *what?*" He yelled it at her, so I slapped him. Once. Backhand.

"I'd love to leave him alone. You, I'd like to be alone with. But that's neither here nor there. The problem is that last night he conked me in an alley and stole my wallet. I want it back." I stared down at him and tried to grin evilly. "Now."

It was Lisa's turn to drop jaw.

"He did what?" she said, her fists clenched on her hips.

"I didn't know who he was," he whined. "I thought …"

"Don't think next time," I said.

I noticed a red mark starting to form on his temple. I began to feel a bit better.

"Just give me my wallet with two hundred dollars in it and then blow town, because your ass isn't worth shit in a sewer. That's a direct quote from someone who knows."

"What are you talking about?" He closed his eye tightly in a vain effort to stop the tic.

"You aren't in a position to ask questions, are you? Just take my word for it, okay?"

Lisa was still standing by the table, her fingertips gently drumming on her lips. She was staring at Blinky, hard.

"Give him back his wallet, you fool. That's all he wants." Her voice was cold.

"But Lisa," he was pleading, "I gave it to … Look," he said to me, "I'll get it for you, okay? I'll get it."

I wasn't listening to him. I was watching Lisa. Something rang softly in the back of my brain. It had the sound of a warning or a premonition. If I had sat down and thought it out I might have saved myself a lot of trouble, but it's hard for me to think things through. I didn't have time anyway, because Blinky grabbed me by the back of my collar and pulled me down. I fell over the coffee table and hit the upright of the couch, which gave under my weight and tumbled me back against the wall under the bay window. He was out the door before I got to my feet.

I would have chased him but Lisa stopped me, or rather, the small-caliber pistol she had taken out of the table drawer did. It seemed to be pointed at my throat, which was somehow more scary than having it aimed at my heart or head.

I looked down at the brown carpet and shook my head.

"You've got to be kidding," I said.

8

"I don't know what this is all about. I think you're crazy, and if you make a move …"

Her voice was calm, unlike her gun hand, which was shaking. I'd never had a gun pointed at me before except in Korea, but that wasn't the same at all. There you could never really see who was behind the gun and you were scared shitless all the time. Here, I didn't feel scared at all. It was too much like a movie. I tried to think what the next line in a script would be after someone said, "… if you make a move …" The only thing I thought of was, "Can't we talk about this?" That seemed terrible so I just stood there looking confused and shaking my head.

Lisa didn't look any more certain than I was of what should come next. Finally, she gave me a look that said, "Well say something."

"May I sit down?"

She nodded her head. I righted the sofa and sat.

"Would you tell me something?" I asked.

"What?" She took a couple of steps toward me.

"Why did you want me to find Blinky? And I'd appreciate it if you didn't give me that worried mother baloney."

"What does it matter? Why should you care? I'll give you another two hundred dollars and get your wallet back if I can, and then you can forget about everything."

"I'm going to level with you, okay? Little Asshole out there is in big trouble. He's playing a game that's going to land him on a slab. Now I don't care about that. I care about me. He's gone and given my wallet to someone. He said so himself. I ask myself—If he was going to merely rob me, why not just throw the wallet away? There's no I.D. in there that would be of any use to him unless he shaved his head a little and gained about fifty pounds. So, I say to myself, he gave it to someone for a reason. What that reason is, I don't know. But I do know that his playmates—that is, the people who would like to see him take a nap on the subway tracks at rush hour—are not the kind of people I want to have knocking at my door, asking me why my name is associated with Blinky's while they're busy breaking my legs. That's why I care. So what I'd like to do is get back my wallet and arrange for Blinky to migrate somewhere where he'll be safe from them and, consequently, I'll be safe from them. Simple, right?"

Her wrist had gradually gone limp while I was talking so that she was holding the pistol with the same thoughtlessness as someone holding a cigarette.

"Well, what did he do that was so bad?"

"Nope. First you tell me why you wanted him found. He's obviously never really been missing—or at least not in the way you said he was."

She walked back to the table by the door and put the gun away. Then she put her forearm against the wall, leaned her head on it, and began to cry quietly.

I should have gone to her, turned her gently by the hips, and softly kissed the tears as they glided down her cheeks. Instead, I gnawed on the skin around my right thumbnail.

She turned and faced me, green eyes moist and glistening.

"Excuse me," she mumbled, then went down the hall to the bathroom. I took the opportunity to go to the table and look at the gun. It was a .22 target pistol. It would be of great use at close range against a stuffed animal.

She came back in about two minutes, composed and pretty as hell. She sat down next to me on the sofa and looked into my eyes. A nice smell of soap reached me. I noticed beads of water on her forehead that the towel had missed. I wanted to leave and never see her again. I don't like fantasies that don't have a ghost of a prayer of coming true. In the best of circumstances I wouldn't have a chance with her. And these weren't the best, not by a long shot.

"I called you because"—she cleared her throat and exhaled—"because someone had phoned me—I don't know who. He said if Blinky didn't give back what he stole, he would get ... oh, what did he say? Um ... oh, yes—'blown away.'" She mouthed the words slowly, as if they were part of some language that she couldn't understand. "And then he said I'd better talk to Blinky and straighten him out—or else. And then he just hung up before I could say anything."

"Okay. Fine. Why did you call me?"

"Because he hadn't come home for three nights and I was afraid, and I had no idea how or where to find him, and then I remembered seeing your ad, so I called."

"So you called me and gave me a cock-and-bull story about a runaway punk and asked me to find him and have him call home so you could warn him."

"Yes, yes—that's right."

"Yeah, well, why didn't you tell me the truth?"

"Because it was none of your business."

"Oh, yeah? So I go waltzing into a goddamn crime war thinking that the job is a piece of cake. Man, I'm lucky I only got whacked on the head with a goddam two-by-four."

She looked down.

"I'm ... I'm sorry about that. I didn't think."

"Runs in the family," I mumbled.

"I didn't know what else to do." She said if softly.

"Forget it. I'm a few lumps smarter now and not really much the worse for wear."

"Please tell me what trouble Blinky is in. I still don't really understand what's going on." She looked at me earnestly as she spoke. It wasn't an expression that suited her. It made her look like a puppy. I hate puppies.

"You have no idea what he's been doing lately?"

"All I know is he's out every night listening to rock bands. I know he takes drugs. I told him a long time ago that if he wants to rot his mind it's his business as long as …"

"… he doesn't bring the stuff into your home."

"I guess that's a cliché, isn't it?"

"I call it 'Every Mother's Lament.'"

"Well, anyway, that's all I know about what he does. He never brings friends home or anything like that."

"Okay. Now listen and don't interrupt. For the last few months at least, he's been involved in stealing electric music equipment from bands that play at AC-DC's. He was part of what looks to be a well-oiled, organized ring."

"But ..."

"Shut up and listen. A few days ago he stole a quantity of cocaine from one of the guys who runs the ring. I guess he figured he'd sell it quickly and blow town before his boss figured out what had happened. Obviously, the goon you spoke to on the phone was the guy Blinky ripped off. He wants his drugs back very badly; we're talkin' thirty to fifty grand." I paused to let the numbers sink in.

"That right there is enough to buy Twitchface a pair of cement shoes. What makes it worse is that Blinky knows all about the hijacking operation and has now proven himself to be untrustworthy, unreliable, and undesirable. And that's putting it mildly. What I'm trying to say is that even if Little Asshole goes crawling back on his belly and returns the dope, his old buddies would be total fools and bad businessmen besides, if they didn't get rid of him in a big way—if for no other reason than to set an example for the rest of their people."

"I … I don't understand." She rubbed her forehead with her hand as if she was trying to push an idea inside.

"Let me see if I can make it simple for you. If Blinky doesn't get out of town pronto, fast, quickly, without any delay, he doesn't have a hope in hell of seeing his next birthday, much less tomorrow."

"You mean they might kill him?"

"Go to the head of the class."

"This is ridiculous. I'm going to call the police."

"What are you going to tell them?"

"Well, that someone is trying to murder Blinky."

"Who? Why? Have they tried yet? How do you know they're going to do it?"

She started to speak but stopped, her breath held. She looked like she was going to cry again. Her eyes locked onto mine as she tensely ran her hand through her dark hair.

"Well …" She leaned over and picked a coffee mug up off the carpet. "Well, what do we do now?"

"We, huh?"

"Oh, I'll pay you. I'll pay you whatever you want. You've got to help me." She was looking earnest again.

"The last time you took an active part in this mess you saved Blinky from the good guy and maybe sent him to the bad guy."

"I'm sorry. I …"

"Don't be sorry, okay? Sorry gets us nowhere."

"Us?"

"Yeah, us. I've got a stake in this, too." I thought about the shoebox sitting in the post office.

"Oh. Your wallet. I forgot."

"Just remember that I'm the doer in this partnership. Your job is moral support and information, right?"

"Sure. I guess so."

"Because I don't want you to get in my way, all right?"

"I don't want to get in your way."

"And also …"

"I understand. You're the boss."

"Right. Okay. Where do you think Junior went?"

"I don't know. I couldn't even guess."

"Great. Good start. Now we're really getting somewhere."

"What?"

"I figure that when you go about doing something and the first step is a total dead end, you've got nowhere to go but up."

"Unless the second step is a dead end, too."

"You I need. Well, I just happen to have the second step right here in my pocket."

I fished out the small black address book and put it on the coffee table.

"Now, I want you to go through this page by page and tell me whatever you know about every name and address that's there."

"Okay. Let's see.…" She started flipping through the pages. "They're mostly blank."

"Well, that's good. There won't be many names to check out."

"It's almost all just first names and no addresses."

"What's under 'D'?"

"Danny, Duncan, and Dora."

"What's Dora's address?"

"Doesn't say."

"Okay. Look under 'N.'"

"Oh." She giggled. "There's just one entry."

"What is it?"

She glanced at me. "I wonder who it could be?"

"Who?"

"It just says 'Scumbag.'"

"Bingo."

"You know someone named Scumbag?"

"I just might. You sure it's on the 'N' page?"

She checked it and nodded her head.

"No address?" I asked.

"No. Just a number."

"What is it?"

She recited it.

"Okay," I said. "Go through the rest of the book and see if anything rings a bell. I'm gonna use your phone."

"Sure."

I walked over to the pink touch-tone Princess and pressed out Scumbag's number. It rang once.

"Nutty Nicky's." It was a high-pitched, whiney voice. "Hold on, wouldja?"

There were voices and rock music and sounds of movement in the background.

"Hey, Sal." He didn't bother to take the phone from his face as he yelled. "Bring the Rickenbacker twelve-string we got in yesterday up from the basement and show it to this guy."

A voice near the phone said, "Hey, Stu, the truck's outside with the Polymoog and some cabinets from the warehouse."

"Jesus Christ. I told you not to have that stuff here till after six. Look at the fuckin' crowd we got in the store now. Nobody's got time to set that shit up."

"Stu, I told Jook what you said, but he said he was bringin' it now."

"Goddammit. Tell Jook he's gotta carry it in by himself and set it up by himself. I can't spare anybody.

"What d'you want?"

"Are you talking to me?" I asked.

"No, I'm talkin' to your Uncle Benny."

A wiseass.

"What's the address of the store?"

"Four eighty-two Sixth Avenue. Anything else?"

"Yeah. I want to talk to Nicky."

"Who's this?"

"Is he there?"

"Who is this?"

"I'm a friend of Blinky's."

"You're ... oh, shit. Hold on, okay? I'll try and find him. Don't hang up." The phone clattered.

Lisa looked up from the address book.

"Well, that's that. Nothing here is familiar. Who's Nicky?"

"Scumbag."

"Oh. Is he ...?"

I raised my hand to quiet her. Someone had picked up the phone.

"Hello?" A smooth bass voice cut through the background noise. "Nicky isn't available at the moment. Can I help you with something?"

"Is this Walt?" I gambled.

"Yes. Do we know each other?" He sounded like a pleasant enough fellow.

"I don't talk to underlings. Just tell Nicky that Blinky's got a friend who knows what's going on and that I'll get in touch with him."

"Whom shall I say is ..."

I hung up. I felt like being melodramatic and I didn't like that "whom" crap anyway.

9

I arranged with Lisa to call my apartment if Blinky showed up. I also told her not to say anything about anything to him and to have him stay put. I left her putting her place back in order and took a bus downtown.

The question about what Nicky did with his loot was neatly solved. I'd seen the ads on TV late at night. They'd show a half-naked guy strapped onto a table with electrodes hanging off his head and body and a huge toggle switch mounted on the wall behind him. A voice would say, "Nutty Nicky's—you'd have to be crazy to shop anywhere else for used music equipment."

Then someone would pull the toggle switch, the guy on the table would go into spasms, and the voice would say, "You'll be shocked at our low, low prices."

I got off the bus at Fourteenth Street and walked over to 482 Sixth Avenue. The storefront windows were plastered with red and black ads screaming the week's specials. The huge air conditioner over the double glass doors dripped water on my head as I walked in.

To my left was a long glass case filled with microphones, cords, portable tape recorders, and other little electric knickknacks that looked like robot innards. Rows of guitars hung from the ceiling like so many price-tagged stalactites. I wondered what it was about them that fascinated kids so much. In my day it was horns. Everybody wanted a trumpet or a sax. Maybe it was the same thing as now; maybe electric guitars just fit the times better. At least you didn't have to plug a sax into a wall to play it.

It was crowded. You could barely make your way into the store, much less get to the back wall where the speaker cabinets and amplifiers were piled from floor to ceiling. They were practically all kids, mostly pimply, hairy boys. Loud rock music was piped in.

A chunky guy sporting a blond beard and shoulder-length hair stood behind the counter. He was wearing a purple Nutty Nicky's T-shirt that had a pink toggle switch printed under the silver lettering. He was asking whoever was looking into the case what they wanted. If they didn't answer right away he moved to the next person.

There were at least twenty purple shirts spread out through the store, each doing a variation of the bearded fellow's act. It seemed that if you didn't know exactly what you wanted, they weren't interested in helping you find out. I figured it was a seller's market.

In the corner to the left of the stacks of speakers stood a desk on top of a five-foot platform. Two people were standing behind it. One had a familiar-looking shock of black egg-beater hair. The other was at least six-five and built like a pro tackle. He looked very serene gazing out over the bobbing heads. He was wearing one of those stupid leather motorcycle caps on his head that the leather boys on Tenth Avenue are so fond of. It had a silver swastika pinned onto it. I gave myself odds that he was Walt and the other bimbo was Stu.

As I was deciding the best way to negotiate the area between me and the desk, somebody pushed me, hard, from behind.

"Hey, clear outta the way, will ya? I'm comin' through and it ain't like I got all day, y'know?" The voice was hoarse, mean, and I knew whose it was.

I moved to my right and turned to look at Jook. He was tall and skinny, with a narrow head and a perfect, dark brown, D.A. haircut complete with a single curlicue lock to the bridge of his nose. His black-rimmed sunglasses, two-day beard, and sunken cheeks made him look nasty as hell. He reminded me of an underfed biker I'd seen in a crummy motorcycle movie, but he came off more like a young thug in search of a spanking.

He was pushing a big wooden box on a dolly toward the desk. I fell in behind and let him clear a path for me.

"Hey, Stu," Jook yelled. "Where do you want this Leslie?"

Stu pointed to the far wall and said something I didn't catch. Jook pushed the thing away. Walt stepped down off the platform by way of a couple of wooden steps near the wall. He was dressed in black leather from head to toe with chains and Nazi doodads hanging from every available zipper and loop. His even-featured face was clean-shaven except for a tuft of black hair under his lower lip. He was handsome in a kind of oversized way and seemed to wear a constant expression of goodwill.

Walt was following Jook across the room so I followed Walt. Jook was struggling to get the dolly out from under the Leslie—or speaker, or whatever it was—so Walt came over and lifted it like it was a box of cotton. Jook nodded thanks and started to walk away when Walt clasped the back of his collar with one hand, lifted him clear off the ground, and wedged him between two cabinets against the wall. No one seemed to take any special notice of this. I sidled as close as I could to hear what was being said.

"Jookie, Jookie, Jookie." Walt was smiling as he gently rubbed his paw in Jook's crotch. "You know I've always liked you. You know I've often defended you when you've upset Nicky with your adolescent excesses." He squeezed at least five lisps into the last two words. "But when you take things into your own hands like you did last night, things that put all of us in danger, I have to remind you that you aren't allowed to do it."

His hand started tightening into a fist around Jook's balls. Jook's mouth was open. He was trying to speak, but all he could do was shake his head from side to side, which caused his sunglasses to slide crookedly down his nose, revealing two dark eyes that were as scared as any I'd ever seen.

Walt's face was relaxed and smiling. The only tension in his body was in the hand that was engaged in mashing Jook's balls. Jook's throat muscles tightened and his face got very red. He was trying to scream. It came out as a loud, dry cough.

Some of the customers had formed a semicircle around the scene. No one seemed inclined to ask Walt to stop. Finally, one of the purple shirts tapped Walt on one of his epaulets. He turned his head without loosening his grip, tipped the brim of his hat, to the crowd, and let Jook drop to the floor. He then courteously pushed through back to the desk and resumed his place next to Stu who had a very contented look on his face as he watched Jook limp through a door marked "OFFICE—EMPLOYEES ONLY."

I walked over to the door and knocked. No answer. I opened it and walked in. It was a small windowless room crowded with gray file cabinets, an old wooden desk, and two chairs. Jook was sitting in one, or rather on the edge of one, bending over with his head between his knees and his hands buried in his crotch. He was swaying and spitting curses at the floor that were punctuated by sharp little movements of his head.

"Um, excuse me," I said.

He straightened up a bit and turned his head to look at me, his sunglasses still sitting crookedly halfway down his nose.

"Do you know where I can find Nicky?"

"Get the fuck out of here." He said it slowly, quietly, through clenched teeth.

"I tell you what—I'll get out of here if you tell me where Nicky is."

He tried to stand up but sank back, wincing, into the chair.

"Hey, man," he said as he bent over again, "I'm in pain, okay? I don't know where Nicky is, all right? I don't fuckin' care either. Y'got that?"

"Where's he live?"

"Who are you, anyway?"

"Would it be fair to say that you don't like Walt? Or Nicky?"

He turned in the chair to face me and gave me a slow once-over.

"You a cop?"

"Let's just say I'm a friend of a friend who wants to make a deal with Nicky."

"What deal?"

"Didn't you just get your nuts crunched for not minding your own business?"

He screwed his face up like he was going to lay on some sarcasm, but thick. Before he could spit it out his expression turned blank, then frightened. It took two seconds for my ego to swell as it examined the awe I had inspired. During the third second a steel clamp fixed itself on the back of my neck, pressing into the hollows above my collarbone and deflating my ego. I spent the fourth second realizing that I couldn't move. I don't remember the fifth.

10

My head was leaning back against something hard. I was looking at an old-fashioned, ornate, five-bulb light fixture that had weathered four or five sloppy paint jobs in its life. I realized that I was sitting in a chair and that someone was talking to me. It seemed far too much of an effort to raise my head to look at the speaker, much less concentrate on what was being said. I closed my eyes and was rewarded with three sharp slaps to the face.

"Oh no you don't, my fat friend." It was a low-pitched, silky voice. "You can sleep all you want later. Now I feel a bit lonely and when I'm lonely I like to listen to people talk. So talk to me and make me happy."

I turned my head and saw Walt sitting on the corner of the desk—swastika, chains, and all. I rubbed my eyes and craned my neck to try to get some feeling back into my shoulders. It occurred to me that this was the third time in less than twenty-four hours that I had been attacked, and each time it was from behind. It was embarrassing. I decided to go home as soon as possible to get my brass-studded sap. If the frequency of assault continued at that rate, I was going to need it within the next few hours.

"I've got the funniest feeling that we spoke to each other on the phone a little while ago." He was twirling a length of chain around a meaty index finger as he spoke. "When I walked in here and heard you asking Jook about how he felt about me and dear Nicholas, I just knew that your voice and the enigmatic phone voice were one and the same. Was I correct?"

I giggled. It wasn't because his question was funny. I giggled because I suddenly saw him as a fruity, leather-wrapped Baby Huey, and that struck me as pretty humorous in my woozy state. He smiled benignly, shook his head as if he was reacting to an understandably stubborn child, and whipped the chain at the arm of the chair so that it wrapped around a few times, missing my right hand by an inch or so. I stopped giggling. He pulled the chain, drawing the chair close to the desk, and leaned over. His face came close to mine. He smelled like strawberries.

"Now, was that you on the phone?"

I nodded.

"Ah, that's better. You mentioned something about Blinky. Let's talk about Blinky."

I inhaled and exhaled in his face. It was more a tired sigh than anything else. He winced and moved away. I hoped bad breath wasn't grounds for a beating. He reached into one of the pockets on his jacket sleeve and pulled something out.

"Here," he said. "Suck on this. It's a Certs. You need it."

He popped it into my mouth. I sucked.

"Now, about Blinky. Where is he keeping himself these days? His old friends miss him."

"I honestly don't know where he is or how to find him." I spoke with my eyes closed, trying to think up a good lie quickly. "I thought that I could get some clue to that by coming here."

"My friend, I have as much a sense of humor as the next fellow, and although I detest braggadocio, I am as smart as the next fellow. You mentioned a deal with Nicky over the phone and again with little Jookie in here. You also mentioned Blinky. Now you claim ignorance. I suggest you reconcile these disparate statements or prepare to enjoy the same pleasures as friend Jook."

He slid his right hand between my legs and cupped my crotch so that his thumb pressed down on my cock while his fingers curled around my balls. It tickled. I squirmed.

"Okay. Whoa. Slow down. I'm talkin'."

"Good. Talk."

"Blinky offered to sell me some coke. I met him last night in the alley behind AC-DC's. He slugged me and stole my wallet. I heard he worked here, so I decided to come and throw some bullshit into the pot and see what floated to the top. I was trying to pump that greaseball—Kook or Jook or whatever his name is— when you came in. I got no beef with you or Nicky. I just want my wallet back and a chance to give Blinky what-for, y'know? That's the Lord's truth."

He pulled his hand back. I realized that my shoulders had risen to my ears in anticipation of intense pain. I tried to relax but I was still nervous as hell.

"You're a lucky fellow, my friend. I believe you. I know someone who can corroborate your account. I think dear Nicholas would be very interested in talking to you. It's too bad he is unavailable until tonight. Would it be convenient for you to speak with him this evening?"

"Yeah. Sure. Why not? Where at?"

"AC-DC's. Around ten-thirty."

"Okay, I'll be there."

"I'll put you on the house guest list so you won't have to pay the cover. By the way, what's your name?"

"Leonard … Howard Leonard. How will I know Nicky?"

"Don't worry about it." He gripped my left forearm

and squeezed. My hand went numb. "Just be there."

"I will, okay? I will."

"I'm sure you will be." He smiled, let go of my arm, and eyed me the same way Lisa had done earlier when I'd felt like a lamp in a junk store.

"Um, can I go now?"

He laughed good-naturedly.

"Go? Of course you can go. I'm not a jailer, I'm a romantic." He laughed some more.

I smiled at him and got up unsteadily. This guy was off his nut. I did want to see him again though. He had made it onto my revenge list. It isn't easy to get on it, but this goddamn faggot had threatened my balls, and other than a few sticks of furniture, my balls are all I've got. He was definitely on my revenge list.

I made my way out of the store and walked to Washington Square Park. It was about five o'clock. The midday heat had abated, leaving a comfortable summer evening behind. I dodged two Frisbees and a soccer ball on my way to the shady corner of the park where old men play chess with pimps on stone tables.

I bought a lemon Italian ice from a Puerto Rican vendor and chose an empty bench facing MacDougal Street. A black couple on the bench next to me was arguing about who should get how much of the yellow welfare check that she kept slapping his face with every time he started to yell. Two leggy teenaged girls in halters and short-shorts walked by, stopping most of the chess games as they were examined, rated, and commented on.

I had a few problems. The game had to be played differently now that Walt and friends knew that I was involved. Going to Nutty Nicky's was a mistake. I had just wanted to see what Nicky looked like; know your enemy and all that. I had to keep Blinky away from them. Nicky would find out about my six-pound theft pretty damn soon and he'd tag Blinky for it. Blinky'd swear up and down that he didn't take it. Walt would turn his ball-busting trick and Blinky would scream up and down that he didn't take it. It might occur to Twitchface that the guy his mother hired might have done it—and boom, my ass would be out to lunch, but good.

Three mosquitoes were foraging through the hairs on my right forearm. I nailed all three with one slap and flicked the mangled corpses one by one onto the pavement. The first was Blinky, the second one was Walt, and the third, Nicky. If only it was that easy.

I walked to a pay phone on Third and MacDougal and dialed Lisa's number.

"Yes? Hello?" She sounded nervous, confused, and scared.

"It's Lenny. Has Junior shown?"

"Um … yes. Yes, he has … but he left right away. I don't know where he went."

"Shit." I tried to mumble it but it came out clearly.

"Well, what was I supposed to do? Knock him unconscious or something? He was mad at me for hiring you and didn't want to hear anything. Wait till you have kids."

A picture of Roxanne floated through my mind. I decided to let her last comment pass.

"Okay," I said, "calm down. I didn't mean, 'Shit, Lisa is a fool for letting him go.' I meant, 'Shit. A good opportunity wasted. Too bad.' Okay?"

"Okay, okay."

"What did he do?"

"He just went into his room and gathered up some clothes into a pillowcase and left." She exhaled shakily.

"I'm getting scared, Lenny. What if they come here looking for him?"

"They won't—not tonight at least."

"How do you know?"

"Because I'm meeting them tonight at AC-DC's at ten-thirty."

"Them? You mean the ones who …"

"Yeah, the ones who. Look, the situation is under control. If anything comes up I'll be at my apartment until ten. You can call me there, okay?"

"Oh, okay. How is the situation under control?"

"Listen, I'm the doer, remember? I say it's under control. Just believe me." I wished I could believe me.

"All right. Lenny, I …" She paused.

"What?"

"I want to thank you for what you're doing." She said it in a thin tone, quietly. "I … appreciate it."

It had been a while since I had heard tones like that from a woman. My legs felt a little weak. I wanted to tell her that I appreciated her appreciation but I couldn't figure out how to say it suavely.

"Yeah, well, you're still paying me one-fifty per, so don't appreciate it too much."

She let out a short, soft laugh.

"Okay, I won't. Call me later and tell me what happened."

"All right. I gotta go now. I'll … Oh, by the way, give me a number from Blinky's little black book."

"Which one?"

"Dora's."

"Why do you want hers?"

The operator cut in with that recorded crap about how the time was up and if you wanted to talk more, to slot in some more dough, Joe. That's how they should say it.

"Quick, give me her number. I'm out of change."

I wrote it on my wrist as she reeled it off. The phone went dead before we could say goodbye.

I was feeling pretty horny as I walked over to and up Sixth Avenue. It was a beautiful evening. The air smelled good, the temperature was just right, and it seemed like all the pretty girls in the Village had suddenly decided to go out walking without their bras.

The brick stoop of my building is flanked by L-shaped stairways. The one to the right leads to the basement, the other to a basement apartment. I happened to glance to the right as I was climbing up the stairs to the front door. Someone was standing in front of the basement door. I leaned over and saw the half of his face that wasn't hidden by the overhang. I could see his nose and I could see the pin through his nose.

He poked his head out and stared up at me. His arms hung loosely at his sides. I started to walk downstairs when I heard a metallic click. It's funny how the noise a switchblade makes is so unmistakable. It really isn't different from any number of things that click, like locks or light switches, but you know exactly what it is when you hear it, believe me.

He held it throwing-style, index and middle fingers halfway up the blade, supported by the thumb on the flat of the hilt. It was pointed at the ground like a long silver fingernail. I kept my eyes on his face.

"Just stay right there." He said it quietly. For once his eye wasn't twitching. The feel of the blade must have soothed that tortured muscle. "It's balanced and I don't miss."

"I believe you."

"I've been waitin' here for more than an hour."

"I'm flattered."

"Cut the shit, man. You said you heard somethin' about me. You said someone said somethin' about me."

"Yeah, I said that."

"What was it?"

"Blinky, listen to me." I tried to get a little Father Flanagan in my voice. "I know all of it. I know about Birmingham, Nicky, Walt—the whole show. I know you're going to have trouble believing this, but I'm on your side."

"How do you know about all that shit?"

"It's my job to find things out. I'm good at it." I sounded like Sergeant Friday from *Dragnet*.

"Why should I believe you?"

"I tell you what—I know something that can save your ass, at least temporarily. If I tell you what it is, will you cooperate with me … and your mother?"

"Fuck her."

My feeling exactly.

"All right, then," I said, "for your own goddamn sake."

"What is it?"

"We got a deal?"

"Yeah, okay. What is it?"

"Nicky told Stu to talk to Dora tonight. He's gonna tell her to tell you that all is forgiven if you sell the stuff back to Nicky."

"And I'm supposed to fall for that? Nicky knows I ain't that stupid."

"Stu didn't think you'd buy it either, but Nicky didn't seem to think it mattered."

"That's your big news, huh?"

"Hey, I'm just trying to show good faith, y'know? Now, will you put that frog-sticker away and come upstairs to my place? Maybe we can put our heads together and figure a way out of this mess."

"What's in it for you?"

"Well, for one thing, I want my damn wallet back. Where is it?"

"It's hid. I couldn't get it if I wanted to."

"Where's it hid?"

"Forget it, man. You ain't told me shit. I think you don't know nothin'."

He cocked his knife arm and backed up the steps.

"Go inside." His eye started to flutter.

"God dammit. I …"

"Get the fuck inside before you get cut bad."

I unlocked the door and went in. I waited a few seconds and opened it a crack. He was still standing there with his knife at the ready. I closed the door and waited a few more seconds. I went out again in time to see him disappear around the corner at full speed.

My first impulse was to chase him. Then what? Even if I caught him, which I wouldn't—I'd be out of breath after two blocks—what was I going to do? Drag him back by his ear? I decided to go upstairs and take a nap. Maybe I'd dream about Mrs. P. again.

11

I tried to sleep but couldn't. I kept wondering if I had gotten into something that I couldn't handle. I tried to balance the risks against the payoff. I'd always told myself that one day an opportunity to make a lot of money quickly would present itself and it would be up to me to recognize it and take advantage of it. Six pounds of cocaine—it was a good payoff, not a fortune, but it would sure set me up for a few years. I had to extricate myself from this Blinky mess before I could even think of converting it to cash. The problem was that I seemed to be getting deeper into it all the time, and at this point there wasn't even a goddamn spark at the end of the tunnel.

I pulled the *Sunday Times Magazine* section from under the trashcan in the kitchen and set about solving one of the diagramless crossword puzzles. It was an easy one. All of the clues had to do with phones and communications, and the diagram ended up being an outline of a telephone. I much prefer the abstract ones that have no rhyme or reason to them other than the symmetry of their shape. But at least the puzzle reminded me of the phone number on my wrist. It was a good time to see what Dora Tired Eyes had to say for herself. I dialed.

"Hello?" Her voice was dull, bored.

"Hi. Is this Dora?"

"Speaking."

"My name is Leonard Hornblower."

"So?"

"I'm a friend of Blinky's."

"Good for you."

"I was wondering if you knew where I could get in touch with him."

"What am I? An answering service?"

"No, I suppose not. Let me change the subject. Was anyone home at Delancey Street last night when you went down there?"

"What is this?"

"This is a game called 'Find Blinky Before Nicky Does.' Wanna play?"

Silence.

I said, "I heard you're a friend of Blinky's. I assume you know that his life could end very abruptly due to certain indiscretions on his part."

More silence.

"I'm asking if you want to help him continue living. I think you might be in a position to help."

"Look, I don't know you. I don't know what your angle is and I don't care, but if you think I'm going to sit here and tell you anything just because you say you're a friend of Blinky's, forget it."

"All right. Fair enough. How about meeting me somewhere and talking? You pick the place. Maybe I've got some things I could tell you. We could trade."

"What things?"

"Let's just say you're about to get mixed up in a nice big mess whether you like it or not. Now, you can meet me and talk and perhaps be forewarned, or you can let it be a big surprise."

Silence again. I was about to drop a few names—like Walt and Birmingham, to let her know that I was worth talking to—when she spoke.

"Okay. There's a restaurant about a block and a half north of AC's on the Bowery called Beefy's. Meet me there in a half-hour. It's six-thirty now. I have to be at work at eight-thirty, so don't be late. How will I know you?"

"You already do. I was at AC-DC's last night. I gave you ten bucks for nothing."

"Oh, you're the guy … I remember you. All right, but if you're bullshitting you won't get the time of day from me."

"You already told me that much."

She hung up.

I cabbed it to Beefy's and got there with ten minutes to spare. It was the corner building and had glass-enclosed porches facing north and west.

I walked through the two sets of glass doors and was greeted by a large-breasted, red-aproned, ponytail-tufted bird. She wore an ankle-length print dress over wide hips. She handed me a good smile, "how-manyed?" me, and motioned me to a small table on the porch facing East Fourth Street. I sat. She handed me a menu that looked more like a movie poster and walked away before I could order a Scotch neat.

The couple at the table in front of me were looking dreamily into each other's eyes over a defoliated chef's salad. Through the archway that led to the bar, a tall, black, gay guy with a large canvas satchel strapped over one shoulder stood pushing quarters into a juke box. The dinner trade seemed to be young, neat, and artsy, with an occasional scruffy type for good measure.

The jukebox was loud and played what sounded like old standards set to a fast, hesitant beat. I'd heard that kind of music blaring through entrances to discos. It sounded pretty boring to me but it had half the people there mouthing lyrics, tapping feet, or drumming fingers against tables. The waitresses walked in time with it, people chewed their food to it, and the cash register seemed to be in tune. Music for robots.

The bird returned, heard about my Scotch, and waddled away. Dora walked through the doors, came straight at my table, and sat down without looking at me.

"Can I get you anything?" I said. She was prettier than I had remembered.

"Yes. A Perrier with lime." Her voice had the same bored quality. She spoke through thin lips that hardly moved.

"What?"

"Perrier."

"What's that?"

"Soda water. From France." She shook her red-brown hair as she spoke.

"Oh," I said. "Let's get to the point right away. The way I see it, I have to get you to trust me before we can help each other."

She stared at my flowered tie. The bird arrived, tray in hand.

"I would like a … uh … French soda water for my friend," I said.

"A what?" She smiled pleasantly as she arranged my drink on a cocktail napkin.

"Perrier," said Dora, without annoyance. "With lime. No ice."

"Yeah, right. Perrier," I said lamely.

The bird dragged out another smile, left, and returned in less than a minute with a little green bottle and a glass.

"Where was I? Oh yeah. You're obviously not going to tell me anything until you believe I'm on Blinky's team. What can I say to make you trust me?"

"Try telling me how you're involved."

"Okay. That's easy. Blinky's mother hired me to find him. Why she wanted him found is her business. In the course of tracking him down I heard and saw various things that told me Blinky was in big trouble. I let Mrs. Perlont know about these things and she retained me to help him get out in one piece. My big problem at the moment is that Blinky thinks I'm out to screw him. I haven't been able to convince him to stand still long enough to explain. That's where you come in. I need you to straighten him out about me. Once he understands that I want to help, he'll have a chance to wriggle out of this mess."

"Why should I believe all that?"

"Here." I wrote Mrs. P's number on her napkin. "Here's his mother's number. Call her and see if anything I've said isn't true."

She glanced at the napkin, picked it up, slid out of her chair, and disappeared through the arch. I sipped my drink and wondered what the hell stake Dora had in this mess. She returned and sat.

"Okay," she said blankly. "She says you're on the level."

"Good. Can you get in touch with Blinky?"

"Now?"

"Yes."

"No. No way. Maybe late tonight, maybe tomorrow."

"Shit. Oh well. What's your relationship with Blinky, anyhow?"

"He's … well, he used to be my boyfriend."

"Used to be?"

"Yeah."

I waited for some kind of explanation but it didn't come. I decided to ask her about something that had been bothering me for a while.

"Can you tell me anything about a guy named Birmingham?"

Her eyes woke up for a split-second and her fingers got busy peeling the label off the Perrier bottle.

"He's a friend of Nicky's, right?" I said.

She looked me in the eye for the first time and spoke slowly. "Peter Birmingham is the lowest scum I ever met."

"Why?"

She let out an unamused chuckle.

"Where should I start? Do you know anything about the rock music industry?"

"Nothing, except some creep last night was talking about A&W men."

"A&R."

"Right. Anyway, I don't know a thing about it."

"Well, I've been working the door at AC's for more

than three years. When I started it was just another crummy bar. Then a band called Telepathy started playing there. They wore torn clothes and could hardly play but they started getting a following. Y'know, people who were sick of all the slick, show-biz bands that were around." She sipped her drink.

"Telepathy played loud—that reminded people what the music was like when they had first heard it in the early Sixties. Pretty soon a lot of bands started appearing and the only place they could play was at AC's. More and more people started coming around to see them. You had the feeling that you were part of a new ... I don't know ... culture, I guess."

"Is this little lecture leading to anything?" I said.

"You asked me a question and I'm answering it. You've got to understand the situation if you want to know about Birmingham."

"Okay, okay. Go ahead."

"After a while the media got wind of what was going on and all of a sudden AC's got a lot of press. The bands got labeled as Punks because they looked like punks off the streets who decided to pick up guitars, and the papers needed a catchy label to pin onto what was happening."

"I never saw street punks with pins in their faces."

"Yeah. That came later when some bands in Britain picked up on what was happening here. They just got more outrageous in what they were doing and started all that safety pin stuff. But that's a whole different thing."

"Oh."

"After a while industry people started coming around. A&R people, agents, managers—they all figured they'd get in on the ground floor and promote Punk, or New Wave—a label they felt more comfortable with—into the next big thing."

"And did they?"

"No, not really. Most of the bands that did put out albums were on small labels with small advertising budgets. And, outside of New York, L.A. and San Francisco, few halls and clubs were willing to book them. People would rather listen to mellow, boring stuff or go to discos for that prepackaged crap."

She was getting fairly animated as she spoke. This garbage seemed to mean a lot to her. To me it was as interesting as the TV commentary after a State of the Union speech.

"One of the people who got involved with the scene was Peter Birmingham. He decided he wanted to manage a band called The Hairdos. They had already released an album on a small label, but they hadn't signed with a manager. He approached them with a contract; they said they wanted to think it over and have a lawyer look at it. Then he offered to fly them out to L.A. to play a few gigs, not as their manager— just to show good faith. They jumped at the chance. They'd never toured before and this seemed like the big time, y'know, flying around the country instead of driving a van to some dump in Jersey."

"So what was so evil about that?"

"Nothing, except that when he got them out there he got two of them drunk and talked them into signing the contract. Then he went to the other three and told them if they didn't sign right away he was going to go back to New York and leave them there."

"They should have told him to go fuck himself."

"They did. But then he told them that he had used the band's name for all the bills—hotel, airfare, everything—and if he left they would be stuck in L.A. with no return tickets and no money to pay all the bills."

"So what did they do?"

"What could they do? They signed and got stuck with a five-year, iron-clad management contract where Birmingham got twenty percent of every dollar they might make, and he wasn't obliged to do anything."

"What do you mean?"

"I mean he could have gone and sat in an igloo in Alaska for five years and still gotten his twenty percent."

"Well, that sounds like business as usual. Worse deals than that are made every day in any number of businesses."

"Yeah, but that isn't all. He got all five of them to sign and then didn't sign it himself."

"You lost me."

"He didn't sign it. He just took it and didn't give them copies."

"So?"

"So it meant that if the band bombed and didn't make a cent, he could say he never had anything to do with them and could dump them in a second and they'd be stuck with a huge debt and he could walk away as if he was never involved."

"Yeah, but they could sue him or something. There's common law contracts."

"But these people are basically just kids off the street. They don't know anything about lawsuits or lawyers. Even if they did, they would never have been able to raise the money to do it. That's what he was counting on."

"So did he dump them?"

"No. As it turned out their first album did well compared with the other New Wave albums. He arranged to have a bigger company buy them out from their original label and then, eight months after he railroaded them into signing a contract they didn't want, he signed it and gave them copies. The new company did a decent promotion of their second album and it did much better than the first, especially in England and Australia."

"Why not here?"

"He didn't promote them here at all. He just seemed interested in getting European and Asian tours for them and pushing the record over there, which is kind of strange considering that a band doesn't really make money until they make it in the States."

"Well, why doesn't he promote them here?"

She pursed her lips and put on a thoughtful face. I wondered why she didn't have a quick answer. I stared at her face. She had high cheekbones, clear skin, and a gently sloping nose. She seemed to get prettier as I looked at her. I looked at her brown eyes, which were staring into the green glass of the Perrier bottle. They were still tired, dull. She was intelligent, articulate, and graceful. I couldn't see her and Blinky as lovers.

"Why doesn't he promote them here?" I repeated.

She glanced at me. There it was again—she was looking at me like Walt and Lisa had done, like I had a huge, greasy pimple in the middle of my forehead.

"That's the wrong question," she said.

"What's the right one?"

"Why does he want to promote them overseas?"

"You've lost me again."

"I guess you don't know as much as you say you do."

"Enlighten me."

"The Hairdos are leaving next week for a tour of South America."

"So?"

"There isn't very much interest in rock and roll in South America."

"So?"

"So nothing. I've told you quite a bit. What is it you have for me?"

"You've told me a lot of nothing is what you've told me."

She laughed humorlessly.

"You asked me about Birmingham and I told you. He's a lowlife prick with the moral fiber of a pimp, and I gave you an example of the way he operates— and it's just an example. He's got his finger in a lot of pies."

"Like drugs and hijacking?"

"Hey, man." She spoke rapidly and quietly. "I don't know what you're talking about. As far as Birmingham's concerned, I just think he's a jerk, okay? I don't know anything about anything else."

Something clicked in my mind. I'm slow, but sometimes I click. I began to understand what she was trying to tell me.

"Listen," she said, "I've got to get to work soon. You said something over the phone about me getting involved in something whether I wanted to or not."

"You know Stu, right?"

"Yes. He works at Nutty Nicky's."

"Well, he's going to speak to you tonight. He's going to ask you to tell Blinky that if Blinky sells his, um, latest acquisition back to Nicky, everything will be jim-dandy again."

"You're kidding."

"Nope."

"Blinky won't fall for that. It's a setup."

"Of course it is. You know it. I know it. Blinky knows …"

"Blinky. Blinky knows about it?"

She had formed the bits of shredded Perrier label into its original shape as we talked. She brushed it onto the floor when she said Twitchface's name.

"Yeah," I said. "I told him today."

"Today?"

"He paid me a visit and offered to help me lose weight with the aid of his little blade. I tried to convince him that I was on his side by telling him about you and Stu. I think he thought it was bullshit. He doesn't think Nicky would set a trap that's so obvious."

She stared at me.

"You don't either. Well, I'll tell you what I think— for free. I think Nicky wants everyone to think he's doing something obvious because he's got something unobvious behind it."

"Like what?"

"Damned if I know. But what I'd like you to do is play along. Maybe if Nicky thinks his little plan is going smoothly he'll show his hand."

"I suppose I have no choice."

"All you have to do is listen to Stu and nod your head yes. I'll take it from there."

"What are you going to do?"

"I'll know that when I do it."

She examined the spent section of lime in her empty glass and sighed. It was an old woman's sigh.

"All right. I'm going to go to work. I hope you know what you're doing."

"You and me both. By the way, are you sure you don't know where Blinky is?"

"Cross my heart," she said, smiling.

"You say Blinky was your boyfriend. What's he to you now, if you don't mind my asking?"

"I don't mind. He's probably the biggest asshole I ever met in my life. Does that answer your question?"

I nodded. She left. I asked the bird for the check, paid, tipped, and left. I had more than two hours to blow before my powwow with Nicky. I decided to take a walk to Delancey Street.

12

The streetlights on the Bowery came on as I passed AC-DC's. A gaggle of winos was sitting in a semicircle in the empty lot next to the club. I stopped and stared at them through a chain-link fence. Years ago, when I was hacking—and hating it—I felt that if nothing came my way I would certainly be a bum someday because I hate to work. I used to daydream about it a lot. I'd imagine quitting my job after a fight with the dispatcher over nothing, going out to get wall-eyed drunk, and then spending every cent I had left staving off the hangover with more booze. Soon I'd be out of money, out of work, and drifting toward the Bowery. I hadn't had that fantasy for years, but I had it that night. It scared me.

Delancey Street was pretty lively. Each corner had either a dingy pizza parlor with steamy, yellowed windows or a hole-in-the-wall deli that featured bruised fruit and broken gumball machines on the sidewalk next to its entrance. Young Puerto Rican thugs were gathered in small groups along each block. Occasionally one would point at me, laugh, and make a comment in Spanish. I was glad I remembered to bring my sap. I didn't like the neighborhood.

The brown van was parked in the same place it had been the previous night, and the door to the building was propped open. I walked in and resumed my place in the shadow under the stairwell.

I waited about ten minutes. I heard steps coming down in a slow, irregular rhythm. Two voices sounded, muffled by the echoes of the noise from the street. They reached the bottom flight carrying a large black box similar to the one Stu and Jook had brought in the night before. They took it outside and shut the door. I heard the rumble of the van's ignition, the meshing of its gears, and the low roar of its departure. I went upstairs.

The wire was still lying along the wall where I'd left it. I wanted to go inside again and give the place a more thorough examination than I had done before. On the other hand, I didn't want to get trapped in that damned closet again by unwanted visitors. Chances were I wouldn't be as lucky as before.

As I carried on this little debate with myself, my eyes rested on a crumpled ball of white paper. It was either a napkin or a tissue. It was lying at the base of the metal ladder that led up to the skylight. It reminded me of Mrs. Perlont's apartment. It reminded me more of Blinky. It had red stains on it.

I took a moment to digest the thought that jumped against the walls of my mind. My eyes followed the rungs of the ladder to the skylight. It was a four-paned window hinged on one side and padlocked just above and to the left of the top rung. I climbed the ladder and looked at it. It looked locked. I pulled down on the barrel of the padlock. It slid open.

I took the lock off the latch and pushed against a pane to lift the skylight. The pane came loose from its molding and nearly crashed to the floor. It was so simple. All he had to do was lift out the pane when he got onto the roof, replace the lock, put the pane back into its molding, and there'd be no reason for anybody to think that their roof had a guest.

I pushed against the other pane, lifted the skylight, climbed onto the roof, and replaced the lock and the loose section. It was the highest roof on the block. A rolled-up sleeping bag, a stuffed pillowcase, a small valise, and a pile of fast-food remains sat about five feet from me near a four-spouted brick chimney.

I had to give Twitchface credit. To hide from the enemy right under, or over, their very noses was smart, daring, and it had worked so far. It must have given Dora quite a start when I'd mentioned her visit to Delancey Street. I had thought, when she had stepped back and stared up, that she'd been looking at the loft. She'd been looking at the roof ledge and he hadn't been there. It would have been nice to know what she had wanted to see him about. It would have been even nicer if she had told me the truth about whether she knew where Blinky was holed up.

I dumped the contents of the pillowcase on the tar paper surface and looked for my wallet. Pointy, patent leather shoes, ripped T-shirts, leather pants, chains, safety pins—no wallet. I unzipped the valise. Two porno magazines, a toothbrush, a roll of toilet paper, two cans of chili, one of beef stew, and a bottle of that stuff you soak in when you get the crabs—no wallet. I unraveled and unzipped the sleeping bag—no wallet, no cocaine, no nothing. One cigarette's worth of deep thought proved futile. A close inspection of the entire roof—including the various pipes, appendages and holes—was just as productive as the deep think.

I put everything in approximately the same order as I'd found it. It was a bit more difficult to replace the loose pane while clinging to the ladder, but I did it without dropping the damn thing. I put the lock back in place and scrambled down the ladder.

I could wait outside for Blinky to show, or I could keep my date with the cruds at AC-DC's. I had no guarantee that Blinky would even come back. There might be something to be gained at the club. I opted for Nicky and Walt and walked slowly uptown.

I came within a block or so of AC-DC's. It was ten o'clock. I still had my list of known facts I had made earlier. I decided to revise it and see if I could get the gray matter moving.

A reasonably clean stoop near a streetlight presented itself. I smoothed the napkin on one thigh, brought out my BIC Click, and tapped it lightly against my front teeth to stimulate some thoughts.

10. Blinky has hidden my wallet or given it to someone.

11. Birmingham is the "lowest scum" Dora's ever met.

12. Dora is Blinky's ex-girlfriend.

13. Blinky's been hiding on the roof above the loft.

14. Dora's the only one who knows where Blinky's been hiding.

I looked up and stared at the pizza oven supply store across the street. Underneath the vowel-heavy name of the store's owner was a list of the types of machinery he sold. One of them was "Dough Retarders." It sounded like a good name for a Punk band.

I reread my facts. They didn't do anything for me. I couldn't see a way out. I was involved in this mess and I had no control over what was happening. I had no idea what might happen. I sighed. At least it was exciting.

A large crowd of kids was hanging out on the sidewalk in front of AC-DC's. Stu and Jook were leaning against the wall to the right of the entrance, talking to a girl with light blue hair and a face like the Bride of Frankenstein's. A couple of hairy Hell's Angels arrived on motorcycles that needed new mufflers. They parked their bikes and leaned on them as they made lewd remarks to whatever girl caught their eyes. Three bums were stumbling through the crowd begging cigarettes and spare change and getting nothing.

Dora was sitting behind her little table arguing with a blond leather-jacketed Punk who seemed to be trying to get in for free.

"Look," she said in her best monotone, "your name isn't on The Hairdos' guest list or the house guest list, so either pay your four dollars or get out."

"Did any of the band members get here yet?" He was bouncing in place with his hands in his pockets. He looked like he had to take a wicked piss.

"No, they haven't gotten here yet," said Dora.

"Well, how about this." He rubbed his nose and ran his hand through his hair. "I'll give you four bucks, and when they get here they'll tell you to let me in, and then you give me the money back."

"Forget it. Either pay or go."

"Aw, c'mon, Dora. I won't have any money left for beer."

"You're breaking my heart."

"Fuck this shit." He ran by Dora into the club.

"Artie." She yelled without looking up.

A bearded, fortyish-looking guy with a chest like a gas pump emerged from the shadows behind the cigarette machine and stood in back of her.

"What's the problem?" His voice was low, but not very resonant, which was surprising considering the size of the cavern it came from.

"Howie just ran in without paying." She still didn't address him directly.

Artie turned and walked through the crowd. He returned in about a minute pulling Howie along in a one-armed headlock. He dragged him through the door and went back to his shadows.

I walked up to Dora.

"I'm on the house guest list."

She glanced up and rolled her eyes as if to say, "Oh. You again."

"Name?"

"Howard Leonard."

"Okay, go ahead."

Walt was standing at the bar looking angelic as hell. I felt for the sap in my pocket.

"Ah, my friend Mr. Leonard. You're punctual. I like that in a man." He tipped his stupid cap at me as he spoke. "Come right this way. I'd like you to meet Nicky. Oh, but I'm forgetting my manners. Would you like some libation?"

"Sure. Scotch. Straight up."

"Maureen." He spoke to the black-haired, black-T-shirted girl behind the bar. "Red Label for my friend. No ice, if you please."

"Thanks," I said as he handed me the drink. "I've been looking forward to meeting Nicky."

"And he, you, my friend." He smiled warmly.

A couple of beefy, bearded guys were arranging equipment on the stage while a third kept yelling, "Hey. Test, one, two," into each microphone.

"It seems much more crowded than last night," I said as I scarfed down my drink.

"Yes. The Hairdos are playing. They're very popular. In fact, they've more or less outgrown clubs this size. They're only playing here tonight as a warmup for their South American tour, which begins next week."

"There isn't very much interest in rock and roll in South America, is there?"

He threw a sidelong glance at me and cleared his throat.

"No. No, there isn't really. Virgin ground, one might say. But that is certainly neither here nor there. Ah, there's friend Nick. Shall we?"

He gripped my right biceps with his huge paw and pushed me through the crowd as he nodded hellos to nearly everyone we passed. I noticed that most of the people he greeted let out little sighs of relief when he went by. I got the feeling that Walt would not win a Mr. Popularity contest in this dump.

We seemed to be headed for a large table parallel to the wall opposite the bar at the farthest point from the stage. We had to squeeze through about twenty feet of packed tables to get there. At one point Walt lifted a chair, with eloquent apologies to its occupant, and balanced it on a table so we could get by. The guy on the chair fell on top of someone as he tried to climb down from the shaky table. Walt thought that was pretty funny.

Four people were seated at our table. Stu and Jook sat with their backs to us, and opposite them, on a bench that ran the length of the wall, were two others, one of whom I already knew. It took a moment for me to place him. It took another moment to glue the memory of a voice to his face. He was the glad-hander who'd been talking to me the previous night when Milky had walked in. His voice had been at the loft. No wonder Blinky'd been so scared when he had looked at me that first time. There I'd been talking to Nutty Nicky like an old chum, and Blinky had taken off like a bat out of hell.

"Everyone"—Walt's bass tones easily cut through the jukebox noise—"this is Mr. Leonard. Howard, this is Stu. Jook you've met. Here's Nicky and our good friend Peter Birmingham."

I nodded and grinned stupidly. I hate being introduced, especially to people I'm trying to con.

Nicky stood and offered his hand to me across the table.

"Hi, pal. Remember me? We talked last night about recording-type people." The tip of his skinny tie dipped into Jook's drink as we shook hands. "Bring your ass over here." He gestured toward the section of bench to his left. "I think we've got some interesting-type things to talk about."

Birmingham was staring at me. He seemed to be about thirty-five or so. His wavy brown hair curled over his ears and collar like a hip talk show host's. The main feature of his face was loose, flabby skin— the area under his eyes, his lips, cheeks; there seemed to be an extra layer or fold on every point of his face. It was an old man's face. For some reason he reminded me of a guy I knew in high school who hated gym class because he'd always get teased in the locker room and developed into a closet misanthrope as a result.

"I hear you had an unfortunate nip-in with a mutual acquaintance last night," said Nicky.

"Yeah. Unfortunate."

"He's not a very reliable-type person. What happened exactly?"

"Wait a second. Let's first understand each other a little bit. I don't know you and you don't know me. We're about to talk about something that requires a little mutual trust. I hear the penalty in New York State for this kind of business is fifteen years a pop, so ..."

"I like your attitude." He looked at me through black-rimmed glasses and smiled. "And Walt says he likes you." Walt smiled sweetly. "I don't know if Stu likes you, because Stu has something to do." He threw a hard stare at Stu, who, startled out of a reverie, sat up and looked confused. A glint of recollection lit in his eyes. He stood awkwardly and headed for Dora's perch at the door.

"Jook," continued Nicky, "doesn't like anyone, so he doesn't count. And Peter"—he turned to look at Birmingham—"Peter likes anyone who he might make a buck off of. Am I right, Peter?"

Birmingham ignored Nicky and kept staring at me.

"In fact, my friend Peter's the type of guy who'd sell you a five-dollar bill for seven-fifty and then steal it back. Y'know what I mean?" He chuckled at his little joke. Birmingham didn't take notice of it. I nodded, wondering where Nicky was headed with this little monologue.

"But you're right about two things—we don't know you, and we would like to trust you. Y'see, that's why Walt's here. If we decide we don't trust you, Walt is gonna take you outside and show you how much he likes you. Walt has an unusual way of showing affection."

"So I've seen."

"I wanna get back to what I was asking before. What exactly happened?"

"In other words, talk or get beat up."

Nicky and Birmingham nodded in unison. Jook and Walt smiled. Artie came over and sat between Walt and Birmingham.

"Artie," said Nicky, "this is Howard Leonard. Howard, Artie Salt. He owns the club."

Artie nodded sleepily and spoke to Nicky.

"This the guy?"

"Yeah, Art. He was just about to tell us some interesting-type things about last night. Go ahead, Howard."

"Okay. But do me a favor. If and when you get Blinky, I want a piece of him. All right?"

"Ha. You got a great attitude. Maybe when this business is over we could talk about using you, y'know?"

"Yeah, maybe."

Birmingham spoke: "The band's going on soon." He said it slowly, clearly. "So talk."

"All right. I don't know how useful this'll be, but here goes."

An electric guitar was making some noises from the stage. The microphone tester was plunking it and then fiddling with the knobs at the end of its neck. I waited for him to finish.

"I've known Blinky for a while. I've bought stuff from him before. Just little amounts. He calls me and says he's got something big and I should meet him here."

I saw Stu walk out the front door in a hurry. Dora glanced at our table. She looked like she'd just sucked a lemon.

"So last night he comes in while I'm talking to you and he takes off looking scared as hell. Obviously, he thought I was working for you or something. I don't understand what's going on, so I take off after him. I catch up with him in the alley and try to talk with him. I told him I didn't know you and I figured he believed me. He said he had nearly three pounds of coke to sell at twenty grand apiece. I tried to talk him down and boom, he went crazy. I think he was coked to the gills. He knocked me down, kicked me and stole my wallet. That's it. Now, I want my wallet back and three minutes alone with him. Y'know what I mean?"

"What did he say about where he stashed it?" said Birmingham.

"What kind of question is that? What's he gonna do? Tell me where it is before he sells it to me?"

"Wait a minute. When I ask you a question"—his face was so flaccid he hardly had any expression—"you give me an answer—not three more questions. Get that straight."

I was beginning to agree with Dora. He may not have been the lowest scum I'd ever met, but he certainly was scum.

"Okay. Here's an answer—no, he didn't say where."

"Did he give you the impression that he could get to it quickly?"

"He didn't give an impression on that one way or another."

"Did he say where he's been living?"

"Look, I told you we argued over price, he went nuts, and I went down. Period. I wish I could be of more help to you nice people."

Walt got up and announced that he was about to "frequent the lavatory." Something by the bar caught Artie's eye and he headed for it.

"Howard," said Nicky, "would you have been able to swing that kind of bread if Blinky hadn't of flipped out?"

"I dunno. Maybe. It would depend on how good it was."

"Maybe if we get to know each other better we can get something going."

"Anything's possible, I always say." I assumed Nicky was thinking about selling me what I'd already swiped from him. I fought a smug smile back down my throat.

"The band's going onstage," said Birmingham. "I'm going to sit closer."

"Nicky"—Jook spoke so hoarsely he was barely audible—"I'm gonna go walk around, okay?"

"Yeah. Listen, if you see Stu, tell him to come find me."

Jook nodded and slouched away.

The band climbed onto the stage from the passageway that led to the alley. There were five of them, including a girl in a leopard-skin miniskirt. The crowd was screaming and stomping their feet. It was strange. I began to feel excited because everyone else was. The din of the crowd combined with the screechy noise of the band checking their instruments was almost painful. But it had a pleasurable side, too. It was almost thrilling to be in a room packed with a screaming mob of drunken, stoned kids yearning to be physically assaulted with loud noise. I couldn't help but get caught up in it. I needed a drink.

13

The first song had started. It was loud. Once I had chased a kid through the balcony at the Fillmore East and I thought the music there was the loudest thing I'd ever heard short of machinegun fire, but in a club the size of AC-DC you had to scream to hear yourself. I leaned over and put my mouth to Nicky's ear.

"I'm going to the bar," I shouted.

He jerked his head back and winced. I suppose after a while one learns how to communicate while a rock band is playing. I was an obvious novice.

I took a different route from the one Walt had

picked. It took me around the back by the pinball machines and then over to Dora.

"What'd you tell Stu?" I was careful not to scream too close to her ear.

She cupped her mouth with one hand and leaned sideways toward me. I heard her clearly. It was a good technique.

"I told him that if I saw Blinky I'd give him the message."

"Why'd he leave?"

"I don't know. It looked like he saw something outside that interested him."

There didn't seem to be anything more to say, so I went over to the bar and was reduced to semaphore to get the barmaid's attention. Someone tapped me on the shoulder. I turned and looked at the salt-and-pepper beard that framed Artie Salt's broad face. He leaned over and spoke to my spinal cord, another good technique.

"What's your pleasure?"

I used Dora's mouth-cupping method.

"Scotch. Straight up."

He leaned over the bar and groped. When he righted himself he was holding a bottle of Scotch and a shot glass. He set one up for me. I downed it and he filled the glass again.

The first song had ended. The screams and applause it got rivaled the loudness of the music itself. There must have been some hecklers up front because the girl singer was making wisecracks about getting undressed.

"What do you think of the band?" said Artie.

"Loud, very loud."

"They ain't that loud. You should hear some of the real Punk groups. Some of 'em are so loud you could

..."

The second song began so I never heard his wisecrack. I could tell it was something funny because he threw his head back and guffawed after he said it. I threw my head back and laughed too. He poured me another drink.

A wild-haired girl walked by and gave me a slow once-over. She was dressed in a red patent leather leotard, purple tights, and turquoise cowboy boots. She was all bound up in leather straps. It looked like she'd been gift wrapped by a crazed pimp. Her face was cute—big dark eyes made bigger by a thick circle of eyeliner, a slightly hooked nose, shiny red lips, and freckles. Her thatch of coarse black hair hung down her back like a Spanish whore's. She had small tits and wide hips and well-muscled thighs. Weird is how she looked, but sexy—in a weird way.

She walked back and forth along the bar. Every once in a while some rhythm from the stage would strike her and she'd do a ten-second frenzied dance that had her head, shoulders, and hips operating independently of one another. The moment would pass and she'd continue her trek along the bar.

Every time she passed me I'd get a slightly amused, slightly curious look from her. Artie kept pouring me drinks. I lifted my glass in greeting each time she went by. After a while she did her St. Vitus dance right in front of me and I started laughing. She looked at me, stuck out her tongue, and giggled.

The song ended. She closed her eyes tight, tensed her shoulders and neck, made fists at hip level, and let out a shriek that would have shamed a banshee.

The guitarist announced that he had broken a G string. I thought that was pretty funny. No one else seemed to get it. Or maybe they'd heard the joke before. My new friend put on a pained expression as if the delay was a personal insult. She came over and looked into my eyes. Her hair smelled good.

Artie handed me the bottle, gave me one of those man-to-man winks, and moved toward the stage.

She stood close to me, examining my face as if looking for some clue to something. At least she didn't make me feel like a big zit like everyone else had done.

"Would you ask the bartender for an empty glass?" Her face was expressionless except for her eyes. They were laughing.

A tray of old-fashioned glasses lay on the bar to my right. I handed one to her.

"I can't afford to buy a fucking drink in this place." She walked away and returned carrying a large canvas bag. She put the bag on the floor between my legs and unzipped it. Her cheek gently bumped the inside of my right knee as she rummaged about.

I saw the glint of a bottle. She filled her glass to the brim and zipped the bag. As she rose, taking care not to spill a drop, she leaned forward; her face and then a breast rubbed against my cock. She stood and took a healthy swig from her drink.

"Russian vodka." She spoke as if I'd asked a question. "Three dollars for a half-pint, but it gets me where I want to go a hell of a lot cheaper than if I'd bought it here. They'd throw me out if they knew I brought it in." Her eyes darted as she spoke and came back to mine when she paused. They were so big and dark I couldn't have taken my eyes off them if I'd wanted to.

"I'm Tory. Who're you?"

"Lenny."

"What're you doing here?"

"Drinkin'."

"I can see that. I mean, why here? You look like you should hang out in an Irish bar or something."

"Someone told me this was a real swingin' place, so I thought I'd see for myself."

"Swingin'? This place sucks, man."

"Then why are you here?"

"Music." Her tone implied that nothing more needed to be said on the subject.

"You like this band?"

"I love The Hairdos. They make me want to dance."

"I could tell."

"I lived in San Francisco for a few years. But I was going crazy there, I mean really bongos. Then I moved to New York about five months ago and I got into all this music that I'd never even dreamed was happening. San Fran is the worst. It's like Grateful Dead City, man. You would not believe it. I was goin' nuts there."

"Yeah?"

"Yeah. I had to leave. I was getting tired of the guy I was living with—you know, getting into stupid fights over little things all the time. The relationship was turning into a big open wound. One day he called me up and told me to meet him in front of this theater to see *Satyricon*, which I've only seen ten thousand times. I didn't want to say no, 'cause then we'd have another argument. So I said yeah, I'd meet him and hung up. So then I called the most insane guy I knew, this painter, right? This guy is so crazy, I can't tell you."

She was swaying back and forth as she talked, bumping the length of her body against mine. Her eyes still roamed as she spoke.

"And I go over to his place and he's got all these Quaaludes and acid. I don't know why I went there. I was just goin' nuts, y'know? Anyway, my old man's waiting for me at the theater and I'm at Crazy Mark's house eatin' downs and acid like candy. I fuckin' stayed there for four days. I don't know if you've ever tripped for four days, but let me tell you—at the end of it your mind and Swiss cheese have a hell of a lot in common."

I nodded. I was getting very horny. Her hip was pressing firmly against my hard-on every time she bumped me. I was watching her mouth as she talked. It was a nice mouth.

"Anyway, on the fifth morning we decided there was nothing left to do but get married. Don't ask me how we ended up deciding on that, 'cause I don't know. We just did. So we dropped some more acid and went and got all the papers and tests and everything. The blood test was a trip in itself, man. You haven't lived till you've gotten a blood test when you're wasted on acid."

I filled my glass again and she filled hers. I glanced at my bottle. I'd already downed about half of it.

"Then we went to this place where people who're going to live in suburbia get married. I mean, it was so fucking *straight*, man. So we did it. We got married. I woke up the next day and thought it was a dream. Then I rolled over and looked at Crazy Mark and I thought: 'Shit, I'm married to Crazy Mark. Oh, shit.' I just got out of bed and dressed and split, man. I called my old man who was totally freaked. He'd thought I'd been kidnapped by the Symbionese Liberation Army or something. He had wanted to call the police, but he didn't 'cause he deals coke, y'know? It's a good thing he didn't. I mean, I really would not have been too thrilled to see cops while I was astral-planing out. Anyway, I called him and told him I was married to Crazy Mark. You can imagine how much he dug that."

I nodded again. She had stopped swaying and was

now leaning flat against me with her back arched so that she could keep her head far enough away to continue talking and drinking. I put my hands on her hips. She leaned her elbows on my chest so she could still sip her drink with one hand and gesture with the other. I really couldn't tell if she knew what was going on. She'd have had to be numb not to feel my bulge against her.

"So what happened?" I asked as I slid my hand along her rib cage and over a breast.

"I came to New York. I mean, what could I do? If I went back to my old man he would have beat me till the cows came home, and I sure as hell never wanted to see Crazy Mark again. So now I'm Mrs. Crazy Mark and I live in New York City and I've got a lot of new friends and great music to listen to."

"How do you support yourself?"

"Well, I'm just about out of money. I work a little—y'know, waitressing. But I got a full scholarship to Columbia Law School starting in the fall."

"What?"

"Yeah, I'm gonna study constitutional law. I did all the pre-law shit in San Fran."

"You're kidding."

"Uh-uh. Why should I kid?"

I was kneading both breasts and doing a gentle grind that she seemed to be responding to. I leaned over and kissed her. She put her drink on the bar and slid her arms around my neck. I forgot Blinky and Walt and the whole sleazy crew and concentrated on sucking her tongue as it glided around my mouth. Three searing guitar notes cut through my passion like a cold shower. She jumped back and squealed delightedly.

"Would you watch my bag? I'm going to try to get

close to the stage. I love the bass player. He's English."

I watched her turquoise cowboy boots melt into the crowd.

"Sorry about the delay." The girl singer's sultry voice exploded from the loudspeakers. "It's the price we pay for those power chords."

A titter of laughter rolled around the club. I didn't get the joke.

"Chuckie," the singer said, "turn up the monitors. I can't hear a fucking thing."

The drummer raised his sticks above his head, clicked them together four times, and crashed them down on the cymbals, starting the next song. I actually recognized the tune. I used to hear it on the radio in my cab ten or fifteen years before.

I took a couple of steps toward the stage and nearly fell. I hadn't been that drunk in years. Someone ran by me, hitting my shoulder and spinning me around. It was Stu. He stopped a few feet from me and looked around wildly. Seeing me, he came up and yelled in my ear. He had no technique at all.

"Where's Nicky?"

"Dunno," I said.

"Where's Birmingham?"

"Ditto."

"What?"

"Ditto."

"What?"

"I do not know." I spaced the words clearly.

"Oh, shit. Fuckin' shit." He spun around, looking frantically. He jumped onto the bench opposite the bar, surveyed the club, and came back to me.

"Look," he yelled, "if you see Blinky ..."

"Blinky?"

"Yeah. I saw him. He's here. If you see him, grab

him. Shit, I don't even see Walt. Goddammit."

He dove into the crowd and headed for the stage. The noise, the crowd, and the smoky air were beginning to affect my stomach. I headed for the door and a clean lungful of air. I remembered Tory's bag and then forgot it; Lisa Perlont walked through the door. I managed to get to her, grab her elbow, and pull her out onto the sidewalk.

"What the hell are you doing here?"

"You're drunk."

"Tell me something I don't know."

"You can barely stand up."

"For Chrissake, gimme a break, willya? I told you to stay put."

"Yes, yes, but …"

"This is all I need. If friend Walt knows who you are and sees me talkin' to you, I sure won't have to ask for crushed nuts on my ice cream."

"What?"

"You know the joke about the genie where …"

She slapped me. I slapped her back reflexively.

"Oh, shit. I'm sorry," I blurted. "I'm sorry. Look, why did you come?"

"Blinky called me and asked me to meet him here."

"Where?"

"In the alley behind the club."

"Great. My favorite place. Did he say why?"

"No, no. He just said it was important."

"Okay. Lemme think." I took a couple of deep breaths that seemed to shake off the haze that surrounded my head. "You go inside and stand at the bar. Don't go anywhere else. I want you where I can find you."

I walked down to the next block and sat on the stoop I'd occupied earlier. I wanted to hail a cab, go back to my apartment, and collapse on the couch. I toyed with the idea of returning the drugs I'd taken from the loft. I almost decided to go back into the club and ask Tory to go home with me. The whole thing was getting too complicated and I was too drunk to sort it out. But there was no turning back. I stood and sighed. The sap was heavy in my pocket. I took it out and tossed it softly from hand to hand as I contemplated the "Dough Retarder" sign across the street. I was sweating.

The air had become hot, damp, and heavy again. Clouds, yellowed by smog and the reflection of the city's lights, had gathered since I'd entered the club. The street had that sickly sweet smell of stale beer and dog shit that only New York seems able to conjure up. Taxis and trucks rumbled over the Bowery's potholes, but that's a noise you don't really hear after you've lived in this town for a while. The constant low-pitched pulse of The Hairdos' music caught my attention for a moment before being smothered by a siren's howl. I walked toward AC-DC's, turned the corner, and headed for the alley.

The shadows of the buildings bordering the alley crisscrossed, making a triangle of light that extended maybe half the length of it. Beyond that was pitch-blackness. It was about as inviting as a graveyard at midnight during a thunderstorm. That was a good comparison, because just as I thought of it, heat lightning lit the sky. I didn't like that either. If I was going to go into that filthy alleyway, I didn't want to be exposed to Blinky's throwing knife by some celestial flashbulb. I decided to stay where I was for a while and hope that another heat flash would light the area so I could at least see if anyone was there.

I was leaning against the corner of the building that bordered the alley. The lightning flashed periodically and lit most of the alley for me, but it only served to increase the darkness at the farthest end where the fire doors were and where Blinky most likely was if he was there at all.

Sometimes I think I'm psychic. A picture of a telephone will flash across my mind and a moment later the phone will ring. Once I was in Boston and I was walking along Commonwealth Avenue when I suddenly thought of a car with a pine tree strapped to its roof. I turned the corner onto Dartmouth Street, and goddamned if there wasn't a station wagon parked there with a small pine tree tied to it. This kind of thing happens to me all the time. That night I was standing at the mouth of that sleazy alley and I thought of a hand. A second later a hand rested on my shoulder and nearly scared a half-quart of whisky out of my stomach. It was Lisa.

"Don't you ever fuckin' do that again," I said in low, even tones through clenched teeth.

"I'm sorry. I'm sorry. I didn't mean to startle you."

"I would hate to have you startle me when you do mean it," I said. "I thought I told you to wait by the bar."

She looked grimly at me and put her hand on my forearm. I turned and peered into the alley, asking myself why I wasn't at her apartment in her bed with her in it. She kept hold of my arm as we talked.

"I did, but it was so loud in there and so smoky, and I wanted to know what was going on out here."

"Nothing. Nothing at all. I don't even know if he's there or not, and I'm not gonna go in there until I do."

"Why?"

"Because young Twitchface threatened me with a knife today, and he's expecting you, so I don't want to surprise him, y'know? I like living."

"Why did he threaten you?"

"Why does he do anything? He's nuts. I'm sure he's been coked to the gills for the last four or five days, so he's probably more twitchy and nervous and ready to do something stupid than he's ever been in his entire life."

"What are you going to do?"

"I'm still thinking."

"Maybe I should call to him."

"Y'know, that isn't a half-bad idea. Go ahead."

She called his name a couple of times and got no answer. I figured that maybe the music was much louder where he was, so I told her to really yell, which she did, but still no reply.

"Maybe no one's there after all," she said.

"Yeah, maybe. I guess we should go find out."

We walked hand in hand in the shadows along the club's wall. About halfway a heat flash lit us up. I dropped to my knees pulling her with me. I felt like I was in a huge Woolworth's photo booth where, instead of getting four crummy pictures for a quarter, I get killed for free.

We made it to the darkest shadows by the fire doors before the lightning flared again. The right-hand door was ajar. The shrill pounding of The Hairdos' music seemed to shake the ground. We stood for a few seconds to let our eyes get used to the darkness. Nothing, not a soul. All that goddamn worry and fright over an empty alleyway behind a sleazy rock club on skid row.

I put an elbow against the wall, propped a cheek against my hand, crossed one leg over the other, and mumbled nothings to myself.

"Well, what now?" said Lisa as she walked around with her arms hanging limply and her face to the sky.

"Now I go and find the bottle I was talking to before you came in. It was a nice bottle, a friendly bottle, and ..."

The band finished a song. Judging by the volume of the screams, it must have been the last one. The shrieks were so loud I almost didn't hear Lisa's from the opposite corner of the alley. Her back was to me. After the first long scream she paused for breath and let out rhythmic little ones that sounded like subway brakes.

My mind was blank as I ran to her. I really should have known what the problem was. It could have only been one thing. I looked where she was looking, grasped her upper arms, and turned her away.

His left eye was open, his right had frozen in mid-twitch. He looked like he was trying to ask a question. Blood dripped down his left cheek in thin streams from his nose. The safety pin had been ripped out. I got out my penlight and knelt. A small hole showed under the diagonal zipper on the left breast pocket of his leather jacket. It was burned around the edges. I parted the jacket and looked at the hole in his T-shirt just above his heart. It was red-black with blood and still gurgling.

My stomach stirred in that familiar prelude to puking. I stood and breathed and tried to relax. I've seen corpses in my time. I don't mind dead bodies as a rule. I saw more stiffs in Korea than most people see in a lifetime. I just hate bloody bullet holes.

I knelt down next to his head and started to go through his pockets. Nothing, not even a spare pin. Nothing in his pants or shoes either.

Lisa came over, crouched next to me, and put her hand on my shoulder. She looked at me steadily. Her eyes were dry, her face composed, but her whole body was vibrating like a ribbon on an air vent. She was about thirty seconds from hysteria.

"Oh, lady, don't crack up on me now."

Inside the people were still stomping their feet and yelling, "More, more, more." They screamed it over and over again, getting louder each time. It seemed like they were the Romans and Blinky, the Christian. I wondered who the lion was.

"Close your eyes, relax your jaw, and inhale slowly through your nose. This ain't the time to go to pieces."

"I can't." Her lips started to quiver.

"Yes you can, goddammit you've gotta."

I cupped her face in my hands and gently rubbed behind her ears. I brought my face close to hers so I could speak softly.

"C'mon. Close your eyes and breathe through your nose. That's it. Relax your shoulders."

I kissed her softly on the cheek and massaged the sides of her neck.

"Okay, now swallow a couple of times and breathe through your mouth."

The band started playing again. Lisa seemed to have control of herself. It isn't every day a mother gets to find her son murdered in an alley. I was a little surprised that my soothing had worked.

The fire doors opened, spilling a path of light and a wave of electric noise onto us. I squinted into it and saw four or five silhouettes in the doorway. I heard voices over the din.

"Who is it?" someone said.

"I don't know." Another voice.

"Holy shit. That guy's covered in blood."

"Who is?"

"That guy on the ground."

"Christ. Somebody get Artie."

"Lemme through goddammit, lemme through." It was Nicky's voice.

He stepped over to us with Walt, Jook, and Stu behind him.

"For Chrissake," he said, "you didn't have to fuckin' shoot him."

I looked up at him. I was still kneeling with my hands around Lisa's neck. It would have made a great snapshot—drunk detective caressing murdered kid's mom while kneeling next to the blood-spattered victim.

The streetlights started to flicker, as did the light coming from the club. The loudness of the music started to fade like a record player's when the plug's been pulled. Volleys of angry curses sounded inside the club. The music died completely. The streetlights went out. AC-DC's darkened. A roll of thunder came from uptown. Everyone seemed to start screaming at once. Pitch-blackness settled over us like a sheet over a corpse.

14

Lisa grabbed my arm and held tight. We stood and backed against the wall. The low-hanging yellow clouds had turned gray. The heat lightning persisted, showing sweaty faces pouring out of the doorway into the alley. I heard Nicky calling to Walt and Walt answering. People didn't seem to be panicking although some were angry that the encore had been interrupted. Most thought that a fuse had blown inside the club and were leaving because everyone else was. It wasn't until they stepped outside into the thick air and noticed that every goddamn fuse in the neighborhood had blown that they started wondering what the hell was going on.

We walked toward the street and got caught in the flow of the crowd. I wondered if I should call the cops and tell them about Blinky. I decided to put off thinking about it until I could find a cup of coffee.

We went around the corner and over to Bleecker Street. Everything was bathed in a dark gray twilight. I looked downtown and saw the red warning lights on top of the World Trade Center. They looked like they were suspended, hanging from the clouds. A couple of winos were dancing on the traffic island that split the Bowery. Thunder kept rolling in from the north as Lisa and I walked arm in arm toward the West Village. She hadn't said a word since we'd found the body.

Someone had a radio. I heard something about a blackout and that Con Ed would have the problem corrected in a couple of hours. I needed a cup of black coffee, and I needed it right away.

"How're you feeling?" I asked.

My question seemed to startle her. She stopped walking and looked at me, or rather, through me. I snapped my fingers in front of her face. She blinked a couple of times and cleared her throat.

"Hey, Lisa, talk to me." I said it loudly.

She ran a hand through her short dark hair.

"I'm all right. I'm okay. I'm just not thinking too clearly."

"Yeah? Well, join the club. I've felt that way my whole life. Actually, it's not a bad way to be. If you do something stupid, you can always excuse it by saying that you don't think too clearly. And it's a funny thing; people are always ready to believe you when you say it. I mean, if you do something stupid and then say that you were thinking clearly when you did it, who's gonna believe that? And if they did believe it, they'd think you were twice as stupid for actually saying it, right?"

She laughed.

"That's the stupidest thing I've ever heard."

"I know. I wasn't thinking too clearly when I said it."

She laughed again, then started to cry. I pulled her into a warehouse doorway and put my arms around her shoulders as she lay her cheek in the crook of my neck and sobbed. She put her arms around my chest and I pulled her close. There's something about holding a woman I like, aside from the carnal part of it, that makes me feel humble and sad and gentle. I've never been able to put my finger on it exactly. All I know is that it makes me sigh.

We stood there for what seemed like a long time. Disconnected, half-drunken thoughts zipped through my mind like cars going under a bridge on a highway. Whenever something about Blinky and the whole mess intruded, I'd chase it out by softly petting Lisa's hair or kissing her cheek. I think I even said, "There, there," at one point.

I'd always wanted to use that great Bogart line, "Dry up, sweetheart." And it occurred to me that this was the best opportunity I'd ever get, but I couldn't do it. I liked her crying on my shoulder. Her warm tears slid off her face onto my neck and down into my chest. Our clothes were damp with sweat and seemed to meld us together into a warm, wet mass. I hadn't felt so mellow and comfortable in years.

"Okay," she said, taking a deep, hesitating breath. "Okay, I'm through."

She reached into a pocket, fished out a tissue and wiped her face. I took her arm and we continued walking in silence.

A doughnut shop on the corner of Sullivan and Bleecker was open. Candles were set on the counter. We sat on two stools near the back and drank lukewarm black coffee.

Bleecker Street was quickly turning into one big party. People were dancing and drinking and sweating like hell. A guy outside the doughnut shop was hawking Chanukah candles for fifty cents apiece. The thunder was getting nearer and I saw some spectacular forked lightning through the window. It started to rain.

It was one of those summer storms that forms huge puddles on every corner inside of two minutes. Dripping bodies crammed the shop while crowds outside huddled in doorways and under awnings. A few hippies danced barefoot in the street.

Someone turned on a radio. It squawked that the reason for the blackout was still unknown and that Con Ed would have the problem corrected by early the next morning. The last comment brought jeers and jokes from the soaking throng.

"Well, it looks like we're stuck here till the rain stops," I said. "I wonder if the subways are running. I sure as hell don't feel like walking home and I doubt if there's a cab to be had."

"I have a car," she said, staring into her coffee.

"What?"

"I have a car."

"Where?"

"It's parked over near the club." She spoke in low tones without taking her eyes off the mug.

"Well that's some good news. It's about time something broke right."

She nodded without much enthusiasm.

I started playing with the wax drippings from the candle nearest us. I rolled it up into little balls, lined them up on the counter, and flicked them at our reflection in the mirror opposite us. It was a little too easy, so I formed my mouth into an "O" and aimed for that. This diversion occupied me until I realized that Lisa was giggling.

"What's so funny?"

"You. You're funny."

"You think this is easy? You try it."

"No, no. I …"

"C'mon. You got something better to do?"

She stared at me for a moment and broke into a smile. Her green eyes woke up a little.

"All right. All right. I'll show you how to do it," she said, laughing.

We each got a candle and set about making little wax balls.

"First man to get ten direct hits wins," I said. "And since I'm the only man, you can give up right now."

"Very funny. Very funny," she said, sneering.

We lined up our ammo, "O"-ed our mouths and commenced firing. I kept cracking wise just before she flicked so her target was somewhat elusive.

"No fair making me laugh," she said, poking me in the side as I shot.

"Interference," I said. "You're penalized one point."

"Like hell I am." She poked me some more.

"Oh yeah?"

I swiveled my stool to face her and let fly a volley of wax balls, scoring direct hits on her face and neck. She responded by balling up a napkin, dipping it in her coffee, and heaving it at me. It struck the center of my forehead and stuck for a moment before falling into my lap.

"Okay," I said. "So you wanna play rough?"

I copied her ploy with the napkin but missed. It stuck to the wall at the end of the counter. She peeled it off and launched it back at me. It got me under the eye.

"Okay," I said. "That's it. No holds barred."

I grabbed her right thigh just above the knee and squeezed hard with my thumb and middle finger. She started hopping around on her seat, laughing and cursing me as she tried to disengage my grip. She grabbed her coffee mug and splattered me with its contents. I let go my hold.

"That's it," I said, forming my hands into a football ref's "T." "Time out. Truce."

She laughed.

"Oh. So you can dish it out, but you can't take it."

"Okay, wise guy. Just for that remark we're gonna walk to your car in the rain so my shit can get rinsed off."

I paid for the coffee and forged a path through the wet horde. The thunderstorm had passed so the rain wasn't as heavy, but it was enough to soak us before we'd gone two blocks.

The storm had cleared the street of people. Walking along Bleecker, east of La Guardia, where it's pretty desolate even on a clear night when there's no blackout, I got the feeling that we were totally alone in a city of façades. The buildings seemed almost two-dimensional, bathed as they were in uniform grayness with only an occasional dark patch where a window or door was recessed in.

I was beginning to enjoy the blackout. It was like a TV commercial during an exciting movie; you turn off the sound, relax, forget about all of the characters' problems, and close your eyes until the movie comes back on and you turn up the sound again. It seemed as if there was no bloody, dead Blinky, no weirdo Punks, no scum like Nicky and Birmingham as long as the blackout lasted. Nothing could be done until it ended anyway.

Lisa slipped her arm through mine and leaned her head on my shoulder as we walked. Her thin, white cotton blouse clung to her body, clearly outlining a beautiful pair of firm, braless breasts. Hershey Kisses nipples showed through the wet material and extended out invitingly. I tried to put all thoughts of sex out of my mind, but—rain-soaked, with her clinging to my arm and the scent of her wet hair constantly reminding me to glance down at her tits— there was no way. I wondered how you come on to a woman whose son has just been murdered.

Her dark green Datsun B-210 was parked near Beefy's on East Fourth Street. She asked me to drive, which I was glad to do. The only thing about hacking I miss is driving around the city at night. I hadn't had many opportunities to do it in recent years.

"Now, how're we gonna work this?" I said as I started the car. "I guess I'll drive you home and then see if I can find a taxi, okay?"

"Lenny, I … would you … do you think … um … keep me company at my apartment? I'm afraid of being alone tonight, especially with this blackout and everything. I don't want to impose on you. I mean, just say no if you don't want to. You've already done so much and …"

She was sitting in the black Naugahyde bucket seat with her arms crossed in front of her chest. She turned her head and looked at me. She was shivering. Strands of wet hair clung to her face. She looked like a little lost child in the glow from the dashboard lights. I hate when women look pathetic. It makes me feel like they're trying to put something over on me.

"Yeah, well, I'm not exactly thrilled about sitting alone in my dark apartment all night either, so thanks for the invite."

"Thanks for being so nice."

"Yeah."

The rain died away as I drove to Fourteenth and turned west, heading for Sixth Avenue. Kids were directing traffic at every intersection. At Fifth and Fourteenth a long-haired guy was barbequing hot dogs over a flaming trashcan while a girl in gypsy clothes handed them out to passersby.

I turned on the car radio. Some guy was reeling off all the do's and don'ts of life during a blackout. After he finished they played some cocktail music, which was interrupted by a bulletin about unconfirmed reports of looting uptown and in Brooklyn. It was almost refreshing news after the lovey-dovey atmosphere in the Village.

The ride uptown was uneventful. I turned left on Forty-second so I could see what Times Square looked like with no neon. It wasn't very interesting. There didn't seem to be any looting going on. The usual pack of scavengers and lowlifes were in their usual places. It reminded me of a Jacques Cousteau film I'd seen on TV where they went down into some godforsaken trench in the Pacific and turned on floodlights where no light had ever been. Weird sea creatures would flash in and out of the beam the same way the Times Square creeps flashed in and out of the glare from our headlights.

I turned uptown on Eighth Avenue. The hookers were out in force, which seemed strange to me. It didn't seem like a good night for business.

Lisa had curled up in her seat. She hadn't said a word since we'd started driving. I tried to think of something funny to say, but I was too tired to make the effort.

The cocktail music gave way to another bulletin. Con Ed promised to have the lights back on by noon; the unconfirmed reports of looting were confirmed; the blackout stemmed from something that had happened at an upstate plant; and alternate-side-of-the-street parking regulations were suspended until further notice.

I parked near her building on Eighty-second Street. José, the doorman, was nowhere to be seen. The lobby was pitch-black, so it took a while before we found the door to the stairs. I fell on the fourth-floor landing and banged my knee. The air in the corridor on Lisa's floor was still and hot. The air in her apartment wasn't much better. She'd left all the windows shut when she'd gone out.

I sat on the sofa and jumped up when I realized how wet I still was.

"Never mind," she said, "a little water won't hurt it. I'll find you something dry to put on as soon as I remember where I stored the candles."

She found a flashlight and disappeared into the kitchen. She came back in a few minutes with a three-pronged candelabra that held long, slender candles. Shadows danced.

"Pilgrim," I said, "your search is ended."

"What?"

"Never mind."

She put the candelabra on the coffee table. Taking a candle, she went into Blinky's room and returned with a multi-zippered leather jacket and a pair of pajama pants.

"This is all I could find. You'd never be able to fit into his other clothes."

"We can skip the jacket. It's too hot and it ain't exactly my style anyway."

"Suit yourself. I'm going to take a shower. You can take one after me if you'd like."

"I'd like."

She went into the bathroom. I took off my wet clothes and put on the pajama pants. I wrung out my shirt in the kitchen sink and put it back on, even thought it was still wet. My belly tends to droop over pants waists and it embarrasses me. I haven't gone swimming in over fifteen years because of it.

Lisa came back from her shower in a powder-blue silk robe and slippers. Her breasts jiggled nicely as she walked into the glow from the candles.

"The bathroom's all yours. I put a clean towel over the curtain rod for you."

"Thanks. What shall I do with my wet pants and stuff?"

"Oh. Here, give them to me. I'll hang them up in the kitchen."

I walked into the bathroom. The shower spigot was one of those modern doohickeys that you have to pull out and fiddle with to get the water temperature and pressure right. It took me a full five minutes to get the water the way I like it. I hate those things.

I stepped into the spray, soaped myself down, and rinsed. I stood with my back to the shower head, zombie-like, for a long time. I heaved a sigh of relief and satisfaction and stepped out of the tub. I shaved in the dark with a Trac-II razor I'd found in the medicine cabinet. I sighed again. I like to be clean.

I dressed and went back into the living room. She had arranged some crackers and cheese and a bottle of wine on the glass coffee table and was sitting on the sofa with her legs folded under her. In the soft light of the candles, the scene reminded me of an ad from a girlie magazine—"What sort of man reads *Playboy?*"

I sat next to her and started munching on a cracker.

"How old are you?" she asked.

"Forty-seven."

"You don't look it."

"How old do I look?"

"Not a day over forty. There's not a gray hair on your head."

"All the gray ones fell out."

"Are you married?"

I stopped munching and looked at her.

"Why?"

"I was just wondering."

"Yeah, I was married once. It didn't take."

"Why not?"

"I make a lousy husband."

She nodded earnestly as if that was a meaningful answer.

"Well," I said, "since we're playing twenty questions, how old are you?"

"Thirty-three."

"Thirty-three? How old were you when you got married?"

"Twenty-eight."

"Then Blinky's ..."

"My stepson."

"Well, I guess I gave you too much credit."

"How do you mean?"

"I figured if Blinky was seventeen, that made you at least thirty-nine or forty and I thought you were pretty well-preserved for that age."

"Sorry to disappoint you."

"What was Blinky's father like, if you don't mind my asking?"

"He was a very distinguished advertising executive who drank himself to death at the age of forty-two, about two years ago."

"Too bad."

"I suppose so. We were married only a few months. He beat me when he was drunk so I left him."

"So Blinky came to live with you when his father died?"

She nodded and sipped some wine.

"Why did you take him in? Couldn't he have lived with a blood relative?"

"He had none. I did it out of some weird sense of responsibility, I guess. It didn't take me long to regret it."

"Must've been hard on you, a kid like that."

"It was. We'd never gotten along very well. He even tried to ... well, let's just say I slept with the bedroom door locked. And he was always in trouble at school: getting into fights, drugs, bad marks. It would have been bad enough if he was my own child, but to have to deal with someone else's under those circumstances ..."

She paused, staring into her wine.

"I know this is a terrible thing to say, but I'm glad he's ... gone."

"You're right. It's a terrible thing to say, but he made his own bed and now he's lying in it. It's no fault of yours. He just took this Punk business a little too far."

"What are we going to do about what happened?"

"I, for one, am not even going to think about it until the blackout's over. When the lights go on I'll decide what the next move should be."

"Shouldn't we call the police?"

"I don't think we should place ourselves at the scene of the crime until we know what the score is."

"But that man saw us. He knew you."

"Somehow I don't think he's going to tell the police anything."

"I hope you know what you're doing."

"So do I. Believe me, so do I."

We sipped wine and chewed crackers in silence. She started brushing out her wet hair. She had to shift her weight and lean forward to do it, causing her robe to part a bit, which gave me a perfect view of her left breast. I immediately got an A-1 erection which was impossible to hide in those damned pajamas. I crossed my legs tightly, folded my arms across my lap, and tried to think about razor blades slicing eyeballs, but she leaned even farther forward. I couldn't resist staring at that perfectly formed mound of flesh.

Finally, she sat back with a shake of her head. I was hunched over with my legs and arms crossed, doing my best to seem nonchalant.

"Have some more wine," she said, handing me the glass.

I reached for it reflexively, freeing my cock. It sprang up, supporting the pajamas like the main pole in a circus tent.

She saw it and giggled.

"Got a problem?" she said, still giggling.

"Nothing I haven't had since I was eleven."

She edged closer, undid the string holding up the pants, pushed them down my thighs, and gently closed her cool fingers around my prick.

"How's that? Better?"

"Lady," I said, trying to catch my breath, "I haven't felt anything so pleasant in years."

I put one hand around her neck and cupped her cheek with the other, drawing her close. I kissed her mouth and felt like I was drinking some kind of forbidden nectar. Nothing should taste that good.

My hand slid down her throat and into her robe. She let out a little sigh as my fingers went over her nipple and caressed the underside of her breast. I wondered the same thing I always wonder: What is it about tits that make them feel so good? And then I thought the same thing I always think: Who the fuck cares?

Her hand was still massaging my cock, sometimes sliding down over my balls and gently squeezing them—a far cry from Walt's favorite maneuver. Her other hand, cool and dry, was curled around my neck playing with an ear as we kissed.

"Would you stand up?" I asked.

"Why?"

"'Cause I'd like to … um … just stand up, okay? There's something I was daydreaming about today that I was sure would never happen. I always think that if you dream about something you want you'll never get it. I'd love to prove that theory wrong."

She stood and faced me.

"I hope you're not going to do anything weird."

I laughed.

"No way. The closest I get to being kinky is necking with girls wearing turquoise cowboy boots."

"All right," she said. "What now?"

The folds in her blue robe reflected the candlelight. She seemed to shimmer. The robe was tied at the waist with a blue sash.

"Now"—I felt a little embarrassed, but a hard-on knows no dignity—"would you untie the sash and let the robe slide down to the floor?"

"Oh," she said, smiling, "you like to watch."

"I love to watch."

"Well, I'll tell you something. I love to be watched."

She started to do a slow strip. Untying the sash she let it fall to the floor but kept a hand on the robe so it wouldn't part. Next she tucked the edges between her legs to keep it closed, crossed her arms, grasped the lapels, and slowly pulled them over her shoulders to her elbows, revealing her small, firm breasts as her forearms passed over them. She leaned over me, gripped the upright of the sofa with both hands, and rubbed her tits in my face. I kissed and sucked and buried my face in the soft skin between them. She stepped back again and let the robe fall to the floor. I just sat back and smiled and fondled my cock, watching her massage her breasts and run her hands up and down her flanks.

She pushed the coffee table out of the way, got on her knees, and pulled the pajama pants off me. Moving between my legs, she started unbuttoning my shirt, letting her tits bump gently against the tip of my cock.

"Now let's see what your beautiful body looks like."

"Mr. Universe, I ain't."

"I'm glad you're not. I like porky fellas."

"Porky?"

"Yeah, porky. You're not really fat, you're porky." She gripped the roll of flab around my waist with both hands as she spoke.

She started kissing and licking my belly as her hands worked on my cock and balls. I was squirming. The muscles in my lower stomach jerked as her tongue meandered closer to my crotch.

She slowly, luxuriantly ran her tongue along the vein on the underside of my erection. I had to clench my fists and tense my neck and shoulders to keep from groaning. I thought I'd pass out from lack of breath as I watched her lips close over the tip of my prick and slide down the shaft. Her hand worked in counterpoint to her mouth. I let out noises that sounded more like agony than ecstasy.

She started to laugh.

"What's so funny?"

"You have some gray pubic hairs."

"So what?"

"I've never seen gray pubic hair."

"And that's funny, huh?"

She laughed harder.

"Okay. The truce is off. It's no holds barred again."

I reached under her shoulders and lifted her clear of the floor as she beat my chest and laughed. I stretched her out and pinned her wrists to the carpet.

Getting between her legs, I nestled my face in her crotch, searching for her clitoris with my tongue. I found it and started licking and sucking. She stopped laughing and let out little high-pitched moans. Her hips began a gentle grind as they found the rhythm of my tongue. She crossed her ankles behind my neck and pulled my hands up to massage her breasts. We stayed in that position for quite a while.

"Oh, Lenny," she whispered, "I'm in heaven."

That cooled my ardor a bit. It just sounded so dumb. I lifted my head and swallowed.

"What say we move the party into the bedroom?"

She sat up, took my face in her hands, and gave me a long, wet kiss that cranked up my ardor again. I got to my feet and lifted Lisa to hers. We walked into the bedroom and made love for another half-hour before I passed out.

15

I didn't know what time it was when I woke up. I'd left my wristwatch in the bathroom. The second hand on the clock on the bed table still wasn't moving. The blinds were drawn. I was sweating. My mouth tasted like the exhaust from an old Buick. The bed still smelled of sex. I rolled over. Lisa was gone.

I hoped she was in the kitchen making bacon and eggs. I remembered that her stove had electric burners so I canned that idea. It would have been the perfect ending to the strangest night I'd spent since the time some asshole spiked the punch at a taxi drivers' union New Year's Eve party with LSD.

I pulled up the blinds and stuck my head out the window. The sun was pretty high. It had to be at least noon. The air was misty and thick. It seemed hotter than the day before. It occurred to me that there wasn't a single operating air conditioner in the entire city. That depressed me.

I took a shower, wrapped a towel around my waist and went to look for my clothes. Lisa wasn't in the living room or the kitchen and neither were my clothes. Even the pajama pants were gone. I didn't like that. I'd seen too many British detective comedies where the bumbling sleuth got stuck in an embarrassing situation because some seductive girl had stolen his clothes.

There was nothing to do but wait for Lisa to come back. I looked for a transistor radio so I could hear news of the blackout. There didn't seem to be one around. I walked to Blinky's room.

The posters that had been tacked to his door were

gone. I walked in. The mass of clothes and magazines that had covered the carpet were gone. The sheets had been stripped from his bed. The leather crap in the closet was gone. Three large cardboard boxes were set against the wall. They were filled with Blinky's clothes and paraphernalia.

I thought of something that scared me. All the things that led me to think it were circumstantial, so I put it aside. Then I thought of something else, something that wasn't circumstantial at all. I went into the living room, walked to the table by the door, and pulled open the wooden drawer. The pistol and the box of ammo that had been there the day before were gone.

I looked into the drawer for a long time, letting my eyes go out of focus as I turned over the possibilities that presented themselves to my mind.

A key turned in the lock of the door. I pushed the drawer home and sat in the uncomfortable chair next to the sofa as Lisa walked in.

"Well, good morning, Mr. Universe," she said cheerily. "It's really hot and muggy out there today."

She was carrying a grocery bag and a shopping bag. The blue summer dress that she wore reached just below her knees and made her look thinner than she was.

"Boy, did I do a dumb thing." She walked into the kitchen and came back bagless. "I decided to go out and have your clothes cleaned and pressed by Mr. Danangelo on the corner. It wasn't till I got there that I realized it couldn't be done because of the blackout. But I got some fresh fruit so we can have fruit salad for breakfast. How's that sound?"

"Sounds good."

"What's the matter?" She giggled. "Post-coital

depression?"

"Just tired. I'm not the young stallion anymore, y'know."

"Well, you certainly were last night."

She went into the kitchen and began doing whatever it is one does to make fruit salad. I followed her in to get my clothes. They were still damp and smelled like a locker room after gym class. I left the underwear in the bag and put on the shirt and the pants.

She spoke: "I put your cigarettes and keys and stuff on the coffee table. By the way, what's that black leather thing?"

"A sap."

"What's a sap?"

"A blackjack. You settle arguments with it."

"Oh."

"Listen, let me borrow your car. I want to go home and change."

"What about the fruit salad?"

"I think I'll skip it. I really want to get into some clean clothes."

"Will you come back soon?" Her voice got small and thin, like a little girl's.

"Yeah, I'll be back in a couple hours."

"Lenny, I'm still scared."

"Of what?"

"I still don't really understand what's going on. I don't know what I'm supposed to do." She looked at the floor and then into my eyes. "Do you know what you're doing?" The green in her eyes was clear and sparkling.

"I think so. I really do. After I have some words with a couple of people, I'll know exactly what to do."

"Well, I hope you come back quickly. I don't want to

be alone, not now."

"Yeah, well, I'll be back as soon as I can."

"Is something bothering you?"

"No. I just told you, I'm tired. I'll see you in a while."

I put on my loafers and took the shopping bag. I was on the third-floor landing when Lisa called down.

"Lenny, José isn't at the door so you'll have to call me when you come back so I can come down and let you in."

"Okay."

It was hot. My clothes were soaked with sweat before I reached the Datsun. I got in, looked at the dashboard, and mumbled a prayer of thanks. That Japanese junkpile was equipped with air conditioning. I hadn't noticed it the previous night. I started the car and switched on the radio.

"… has been restored in Dutchess and Westchester counties and parts of the Bronx and Long Island. Spokesmen at Con Edison are confident that power will be restored to the entire metropolitan area by early this evening."

I drove east to Seventh and headed downtown.

"The widespread looting of last night and early this morning seems to have ended. Mass arrests have been made but police officials say the arrests represent only a fraction of the looting committed. Neither the police nor the mayor's office was willing to estimate the cost of the looting, but one City Hall official told me, and I quote, 'It's going to cost millions. There's going to be a lot of places put out of business for good. Those people acted like animals.' The official asked not to be named. Mayor Beame has issued an appeal to …"

I turned off the radio. The police must have been very busy with the looting and the blackout. I wondered if anyone had notified them about a corpse on the Bowery.

I set the air conditioner on high. In five minutes the car was so cold I had to turn it down. The sweaty clothes became cool, almost icy against my skin.

I parked the car in a lot on Thirty-first Street and took the bag of underwear to my apartment. I wondered if the phones were out too. I picked up the receiver and heard the dial tone.

I put on some clean underwear, a pair of tan double knits, and a light blue shirt. Picking up an unfinished crossword puzzle, I settled on the couch and gave it my full concentration. It didn't take long to finish. I made myself a couple of warm cheese and limp lettuce sandwiches and decided to head back to Lisa's.

On my way to the parking lot I changed my mind because I got an urge to look at an alley downtown. I drove east and went downtown on Second Avenue.

The Bowery was steamy and uninviting. I slowed to a crawl as I passed the mouth of the alley. I don't know what I'd expected to see: maybe police cars and an ambulance, maybe the rain-soaked corpse still lying there. What I didn't expect to see was nothing—which was exactly what was there.

I parked and walked into the alley. There was a set of tire tracks in the muck. They led right to where the body had been. I knelt in the same spot I'd been in the night before when I'd gagged at the sight of the blood. There was no blood there now, not a trace. It had been washed away by the rain or maybe someone had sopped it up, or both.

I played with the idea that maybe the cops had been there and gone already. I didn't play with it for long. They would have cordoned off the alley and still been hanging around. I had to be sure though. I had to be sure the cops hadn't been there. Once I had seen a guy get clipped by a truck on Twenty-third and Seventh. I walked into a deli on the corner, ordered a sandwich, and when I came back out they'd already peeled the guy off the pavement and carted him away. It looked like nothing had happened there. That's how it looked in the alley. I walked around the corner to the flophouse.

One of my drinking buddies from two days before was sitting shirtless on the tiled floor of the foyer. It was the runt with the phlegm-tone voice.

"Hello, friend."

He looked up at me. The whites of his eyes were yellowed and streaked red with forked blood vessels. His breathing was labored and wheezy.

"Hello, friend," I repeated.

He opened his mouth but nothing came out. His tongue was white. He was dehydrated, dry as a bone. The man needed a drink to get straight. He needed it bad.

I walked to the liquor store, bought some wine, brought it back, and handed him the bottle. He gulped some down but coughed it back out. It brought him around though. He started taking small sips. His lips and hands were quivering.

"I'm alcoholic," he said, clutching the bottle.

"I could tell."

"An' you come an' gimme dis wine."

"Yeah. I did that."

"I'm gonna"—he sat up a little straighter—"I'm a-gonna sing for you 'cause you be givin' me dis wine."

"I don't want you to sing. I want to know …"

His voice was raspy but not flat. His selection was "Pennies from Heaven," which I thought was apt. He sang it at a slow tempo, taking deep breaths between phrases and drawing out the last syllable of each phrase in a tremolo that reminded me of Louis Armstrong.

By the end of the first chorus he was gesturing with his hands. By the end of the song he was really belting it out. When he finished I gave him a dollar, which he kissed and tucked into his shoe.

"Look, friend, before you get to 'Over the Rainbow,' I want you to tell me something."

He took another slug from the bottle.

"I don' know dat one."

"Good. Listen to me."

I took away the bottle, which gained me his undivided attention.

"Did you see a lot of cops around here today?"

"Say what?"

"Cops—did you see any this morning?"

"Hell ain't been no police here. I'd of seen 'em. If they be comin' around here, I'd of seen 'em. I can smell policemens."

"You sure?"

"Sure as you be holdin' dat bottle. I been settin' here since befo' de lights go an' dey ain't been no police."

I gave him back the bottle and walked back to the alley. One problem was solved. I wasn't about to call the cops and tell them about a murdered Punk who wasn't there.

I went to where the body had been and tried to figure out what the hell was going on. The fire doors opened. Artie Salt stepped into the alley.

"What're you hanging around here for?" He didn't seem to remember me. "Get out."

"Howard Leonard, Mr. Salt," I said, offering my hand. "We met last night."

He looked me up and down, ignoring my hand. "Oh yeah. How ya doin'? Get out."

"Sure, sure. I don't want to be here anyway. I was just passing by and I noticed that this place looked a little emptier than it did last night."

"What's that supposed to mean?" He stepped closer. He smelled of booze.

"Nothing."

"Then get out of here before I lose my foot up your ass."

I went.

I walked to Beefy's. It was closed "due to blackout." There probably wasn't a cool drink to be had in the whole city on the hottest goddamn day of the year. Nothing to do but drive back to Lisa's.

"Blinky's dead" —the thought just kept running through my mind as I drove uptown. I suddenly realized that there was nothing holding me anymore. The one person who might've guessed that I took Nicky's dope was dead. I didn't care who killed him. I didn't care who moved the body. I was home free.

I called Lisa from a pay phone on West End Avenue. She was waiting at the door when I got to her building.

"Lenny, Lenny." She looked nervous as hell. "The police just called. They called and asked me to go to the precinct house."

"Which one?"

"They said it was on Twentieth Street between Seventh and Eighth. Lenny, I'm scared."

"Let's go upstairs and talk. They probably want you to identify the body."

"I don't want to. Lenny, I don't want to go."

"Well, you're going to have to, so you might as well not get crazy about it. C'mon upstairs."

The apartment was as hot and muggy as the air

outside. We sat on the sofa. I took off my shoes and socks and unbuttoned my shirt.

"Listen to me, Lisa. Did anyone see you leave here last night?"

"No. No, I don't think so."

"Good. You're going down there. They're going to break the news about Blinky."

"They told me over the phone."

"Heartless bastards. How did you react?"

"I was so shocked that it was the police, I didn't say anything. I didn't even say goodbye."

"Good. Perfect. Okay, when they ask about Blinky, you tell the truth. Don't lie. But just don't tell them about going down to AC-DC's last night. Don't tell them about me. Everything else is fine: he was missing; you were worried; you got a threatening phone call; you didn't know what to do; Blinky came home yesterday, took some stuff, left without a word; you don't know anything about drugs."

"Won't they ask about AC-DC's?"

"No."

"Why not?"

"Because they didn't find the body there."

"What?"

"Someone moved it. They must have dumped it in Chelsea somewhere. That's why they want you to go to that precinct."

"Why would anyone do that?"

"Let me put it to you this way: if you owned a club and were involved in hijacking, drugs, and God knows what else, would you want a murder victim in your backyard?"

"You mean someone from AC-DC's moved him?"

"It's as good a theory as any other. It doesn't matter anyway. What matters is that you tell the police only what I told you to tell them. Remember, you don't have to lie; just don't tell them the whole truth. The whole truth makes us both suspects in a murder case and you wouldn't want that, would you?"

"No, no, of course not." She ran a hand through her hair and wiped a bead of sweat from her forehead. "I don't know if I can do this."

"You don't have a choice. It'll be over before you know it. They don't give bereaved mothers the third degree unless they have a reason to. That's your job; don't give them a reason."

She sat back and let out a long sigh.

"When do they want you down there?"

"As soon as possible."

"Well, you might as well get it over with."

"Will you come? Will you drive me down?"

"Sure. I'd rather sit in an air-conditioned car than in this steam bath."

She put her hands to my cheeks and gave me a long, soft kiss.

"You're a godsend," she whispered. "I don't know what I would have done without you." She locked her eyes to mine and kept them there for a long moment.

She looked earnest again. I didn't like that expression on her, but it was better than the pathetic one.

We got ready, went to the Datsun, and drove downtown.

"… looting continues. Earlier reports that the police had it under control were apparently false. Con Edison spokesmen now place the blame for the power outage on severe lightning storms upstate that struck major power lines. There are also unconfirmed reports of malfunctions in a transformer station. Con Edison has announced that power will be restored to the entire metropolitan area by midnight tonight. It is now four-thirty P.M. More news after …"

I parked the car on Seventh Avenue just above Twentieth Street.

"I'll wait here," I said, "Don't worry. Just remember what I told you."

"Okay. Okay, I will. I just wish that you could come with me."

She got out and walked around the corner. I felt the rumble of the subway beneath me. At least that was working.

Everything seemed to be going along fine. The police would investigate, find the killer or not find him, and I could concentrate on converting the coke to cash. I tore up my list of facts and threw it out the window. The car was getting hot so I turned on the engine and set the air conditioner on low.

The missing pistol and Blinky's packed clothes bothered me. The scary thought passed through my mind again. I decided to ignore it unless and until something happened to substantiate it.

I turned my thoughts to more pleasant business like my future apartment. The living room'd look like one of those modern apartments in the back of the *Times Magazine* section—no paintings or posters on the walls, a low black couch with a square metal-and-glass table in front of it, and big black cushions thrown on the floor with tasteful arbitrariness. The billiard room would be the classic British type with the low-hanging light fixture above the table. The table would have to have green felt—none of this blue or gold crap that you see in pool halls these days. It'd have to have thick wooden legs and tassels hanging from the pockets. And it had to be regulation size. I hate those tiny bar tables.

I really didn't know how the bedroom should look. I'm not big on bedrooms. You sleep there so why bother to decorate it if your eyes are going to be closed? One thing, though: I'd hire someone to come in once a week to change the sheets. That'd be a must. I hate making beds.

Lisa opened the door, plopped into the bucket seat, and stared at me. I waited for her to say something. She didn't.

"Well?"

Silence.

"C'mon. What happened?"

She looked scared.

"What happened? Don't just sit there like a goddamn showroom dummy."

"They asked me about you."

She kept staring at me. Her fingers dug into her thighs.

"Don't joke with me. What happened?"

"I'm telling you—I'm telling you what happened." She gripped the dash above the glove compartment and turned to face me. "They had him in an ambulance and they showed him to me and I said it was him. Lenny, his eyes were still open. I almost threw up. Then they asked me his age and stuff like that, and then they wanted to know if I've ever heard of you."

I pictured a pool table in flames. I cleared my throat. "Did they say why?"

"They found a wallet on the ground near him. It was your wallet."

It figured. I was so busy signing the lease for my new apartment, I'd forgotten about the goddamn wallet. Damn kid had a hand on me even from the grave.

"What did you tell them?"

"I told them I never heard of you. That's what you said I should say."

"Yeah, that's what I said, only I didn't figure on this. Now you've lied to them. Who knows? Maybe it's the best thing that could have happened."

"How do you mean?"

"I haven't the slightest idea. I'm trying to look on the bright side."

We sat in silence for a few minutes. I chewed on the skin around my left thumbnail. She played with a button on her shirt.

"How did they know it was Blinky?"

"They had his fingerprints on file from when he was arrested for selling pot last year."

"This is great. This is just dandy. It's funny. A minute ago I was congratulating myself on getting out of this thing in one piece. Now I'm the number one suspect in a murder case."

"How could they suspect you? Just because your wallet was there doesn't mean …"

"They like to wrap murders up fast, especially ones that aren't going to make the papers. You've got a dead kid with an arrest record, no blood relatives, no motive for his death, nobody gives a shit if his murderer is found—not even you. Am I right?"

She started to speak but stopped.

"So if they're handed a clue like my wallet on a silver platter, they jump on it and they don't care if it's a plant or not. People saw me chase him the other night. And a bunch of people, maybe even some who saw me chase him, saw me leaning over his body. Shit. If the cops put that much together they'll indict me in a second."

"Well, what are you going to do?"

"I suppose I could go to the cops and try and explain

everything, or …"

"Or what?"

"Or I can try and find the killer myself."

16

"What good is that going to do?"

"I'm not quite sure. It sounded good. I just know that I'm not going to go to the cops on my own. They'd either arrest me or hold me as a material witness and I've got nothing to offer to clear myself."

"You could tell them about those men who were after him."

"I haven't got a shred of proof. All those guys'd have to do is deny it and say I'm nuts and who's to say they're wrong. It'd be my word against five of them."

"You could tell the police about those drugs and the hijacking and everything."

"Yeah, I could do that, but I won't. Look what happened to Blinky. I like living."

"The police could protect you, couldn't they?"

"I suppose they could, but I got other reasons too."

"What reasons?"

"Lisa, where's the gun?"

"What gun?" She looked like I'd just kicked her in the ass.

"The gun that you waved at me yesterday."

"It's still there in the drawer."

"No it isn't."

"Well, I don't know where it is." Her eyelids closed and opened the way mine do when something clicks in my brain. "What are you trying to say?"

"Nothing. I'd just like to know where the gun is."

"I don't know where it is. How the hell should I

know?" She was starting to yell. She was almost as good as Tory.

"For Chrissake, don't get mad."

"Don't get mad? Don't get mad? After everything that's happened in the last twenty-four hours, all I've been through, after what happened between us last night, and you say don't get mad?"

"Could you hold it down a bit?"

"Hold it down? Hold it down?"

She was better than Tory. A couple of notes higher and she'd be out of range of human hearing. I looked around, half-expecting every dog in the neighborhood to be coming toward the car.

"I go into the goddamn police station and lie for you, and here you are asking me about the gun and saying I k-killed Blinky and you tell me to keep it down?"

"I didn't say you killed anybody."

"Well, you might as well have. Maybe I'll just go back to the police and tell them exactly who you are and where you are. Why shouldn't I? Why shouldn't I make it easier for them?"

I put the car into gear and took off. She kept jabbering all the way uptown. I figured she'd been under a lot of stress, so I shut up and drove. She was considerate enough to yell at just below the pain threshold. By the time we parked near her apartment, she had me ranked with Adolf Hitler, Lee Harvey Oswald, and Son of Sam as the four biggest male swine of the twentieth century.

"Did José see you leave last night?" I asked as we walked to her building.

She nodded without looking at me.

"Did the cops ask you where you were last night?"

She shook her head.

"So?" she asked.

"So, if the cops ask you where you were, you better have a nice story, because José saw you leave and no one was here to see when you came back."

"Why should they ask that?"

"I don't know, but they're gonna talk to you again. They're gonna want to know a lot of things."

We entered the apartment. I didn't see them at first because I turned to close the door. Lisa let out a little shriek, backed up, and knocked my head against the door.

Nicky and Jook were sitting on the sofa. Walt's huge frame dwarfed the chair. Jook's feet were on the glass tabletop. He was chewing gum. Walt was smiling pleasantly and twirling his leather cap around one finger. Nicky had a big black .45 pointed in our general direction.

"Hi, pal," said Nicky. "I don't know why, but I expected to find you here. You seem to turn up everywhere."

"Lenny, who are these people?" She said it through the side of her mouth.

"These nice fellas are some of Blinky's pals."

"Hey, Nick." Jook was hoarse as ever. He spoke between chews. "She ain't bad. I'd sure like to park my pud in her garage, haw-haw."

Walt reached over and flicked Jook's face with the back of his hand. From a normal human it would have been a light tap. Jook's head snapped back like he'd just leaned into an uppercut.

"Your manners, friend Jook, are as appalling as your personal hygiene." Walt kept smiling as he spoke. "I suggest you give your seat to the lady."

He grabbed Jook's shirt and flung him onto the

carpet by the kitchen door. Jook got up and pointed an index finger at Walt.

"One day I'm gonna fuckin' …"

"Shut up, shithead," said Nicky.

"Mrs. Perlont"—Walt motioned to the vacant part of the sofa next to Nicky—"please sit here."

She looked at me.

"When that guy asks you to do something"—I tilted my head toward Walt—"do it."

"Excellent advice, my dear Howard," Walt said as Lisa sat. "Oh, but it isn't Howard, is it? Nicky, what's his name?"

"Hornblower. Leonard Hornblower. Stupid Hornblower is what it should be, leavin' his wallet next to the guy he killed. Boy, are you ever dumb."

I smiled weakly.

"And now … what'd you call him?" He glanced at Lisa. "Oh, yeah. Now, Lenny, I want to hear your story all over again. I decided I didn't like the one you told me last night. I want to hear one that ends with you comin' in here with Blinky's mom and it's gotta include you and her in that alley last night. What else? Oh yeah. I found out something today that really upset me. It upset me twice as much as when I found out I was missing three pounds of blow. I want you to work that in too."

He released the safety on the automatic, put his feet on the table, rested his left arm across his bent knees, and supported his gun wrist on his left elbow. If he aimed at my head, the recoil would throw the bullet too high because you've got to hold your wrist with a gun that size, not just support it. If he aimed at my stomach he'd probably blow a half-dollar-size hole through my throat. He aimed at my stomach.

I tried to think up a lie that'd cover all the stuff he

DEATH OF A PUNK

mentioned, but he wanted me to start talking right away. I decided to take the advice I gave to Lisa and tell him the truth, leaving out anything that might result in a hole in my throat.

"All right. Don't get upset. I like living," I said.

I didn't like the way he was peering down the barrel of the gun.

"Mrs. Perlont called me up and asked me to find Blinky. I never heard or saw either of them before she called me four days ago. She gave me some bullshit story and I went for it. All she wanted was for him to call home so she could warn him about the phone call you gave her, which is something I found out later. I went to AC-DC's—that was the night I met you—and he showed up. I caught up with him in the alley. He thought I was after him because I was working for you; he'd seen us sitting together. He didn't give me a chance to open my mouth. He took my wallet, which had the two-hundred-dollar retainer his mother had given me. I overheard this jerk"—I nodded toward Jook—"talking to the other jerk about how Blinky was in big trouble with Nicky and about stolen coke, so I put two and two together and figured the best way to find Blinky and get my wallet and money back was to somehow get in with you guys, because I figured you'd find him for me quicker than I'd find him myself."

I stopped for breath. He made a little motion with the gun that said, "Keep talkin'."

"Then last night, Mrs. P. there comes into the club and says that Blinky called her and asked her to meet him in the alley. We went back there, found the body, you showed up, and the lights blew. We came back here. The cops called today and I drove her downtown to talk to them. They found the body and my wallet somewhere in Chelsea. They wanted her to make a positive I.D. of Blinky. She didn't tell them anything about you because she don't know anything about you. Then we came back here and found you lovely gentlemen."

If he didn't believe that, I was out of luck, because I didn't have any stories left. I wiped away the sweat that was streaming down my face.

"That's good. Ain't that good, Walt?"

"He speaks persuasively. He does indeed. No doubt about that."

"You believe him?"

"Not at all. I find him a shade too glib for my taste."

"Yeah, I feel the same way. Lenny, you left something out. You left out the part about how you and Blinky were in business together to sell my blow and how he got mad at you for trying to double-cross him and how he stole everything I had left the next day and how you shot him in the alley. You left all that stuff out and that's what I wanted to hear. But what I really want to hear is where the shit is now. I want to hear that so bad I can taste it. So why don't you just come out with it?"

I inhaled and exhaled loudly.

"Look," I said, "I never laid eyes on Blinky before that night, and I can prove it."

"How?"

"I have a tape of Mrs. Perlont's call to me when she hired me. I always tape clients when they first call so I have a reference for details. That tape is sitting in my apartment. The problem is that I can't go back there because the cops are looking for me because of that goddamn wallet."

"If all that's true, why'd you kill the kid?"

"Y'know, I'm getting tired of hearing you say that. What makes you so sure ..."

He moved the gun a little to the left and fired. I jumped. I mean that scared the living shit out of me. There's no sensation quite like seeing a gun that's pointed at you go off and then opening your eyes to find that you haven't been hit.

"Don't ask questions. I ask the questions."

"Man"—I leaned back against the wall near the bullet hole—"please, don't do that. I won't ask any more questions. I'll say what you want me to. Just don't do that."

"Now that's the type of stuff we like to hear, ain't it, Walt?"

"I believe he's genuinely frightened. It suits him. Portly men seem to enjoy being frightened."

I almost told him I was porky, not portly, but I wasn't about to speak anymore unless spoken to.

"Walt, what do you think about this tape stuff?"

"It strikes me, Nicholas, that it's not the type of stuff that lies are made of. It wouldn't really be practical to go to his apartment, even if the constabulary wasn't there, so we cannot verify the veracity ..."

"Cut the shit, Walt. Do you believe him?"

"In a word, yes."

"Yeah, I kinda do, too. Maybe he really don't know nothin'. But you know what I think is an interesting-type thing? I think it's interesting that Blinky's mom, of all people, should be at the club last night. And if what ole Lenny says is right, she went there because Blinky told her to. Now, that makes me wonder."

Walt's eyes lit up a little. He turned to face Lisa.

"Now, Mrs. Perlont, my friend Nicky is going to ask you some questions. Please don't be afraid, unless you lie—then you can be afraid."

"Yeah," said Nicky. "Walt's never hurt a woman. He

mostly likes boys, but I think he wouldn't mind making an exception in your case."

Lisa was sitting up straight with her hands in her lap. She didn't look nervous. She looked expectant.

"First of all"—Nicky fiddled with his skinny tie with one hand; the other was occupied with aiming the cannon at me—"where's the coke?"

"What coke?"

"Walt," said Nicky.

Walt grabbed a handful of Lisa's hair and wound it around his fist, nearly lifting her off her seat. Nicky looked bored. Jook was smiling. I looked at the floor and waited for Lisa to scream or cry or both.

She didn't scream or cry. I glanced at them. She was hanging from Walt's paw like a punching bag. She looked calm as hell.

"Well?" said Nick.

"Tell this overblown queer to let go of me and maybe we can talk."

Nicky nodded at Walt. He dropped her back on the sofa as my jaw dropped to the floor.

"Okay," said Nicky. "Talk."

"What's it worth to you?"

"Lady, I didn't come here to play 'Let's Make a Deal.'"

"You can beat me and I won't tell you a thing, or you can kill me and then you'll never get anything."

"Walt, she thinks we're kidding," he sighed.

Nicky's eyelids drooped lazily. He pivoted a little and socked her in the mouth. Blood ran out of her upper lip and dribbled down her chin.

"My husband did better than that when he was so drunk he could hardly stand."

"You're probably right. I was never very good at this interrogation-type stuff." He licked his knuckles. "Walt, enjoy yourself."

Walt tucked a hand into her armpit, lifted her over the coffee table, and set her down in the middle of the room. He stared her up and down, trying to decide the best way to go about it. He pulled her a little closer. He reached for her with his free hand. She kicked him in the nuts. It was so fast I didn't realize what had happened until he bent over and groaned. It must have been a hell of a kick because his crotch was at her chest level.

He kept hold of her while he fought off the pain. Jook and Nicky seemed to be enjoying the show. Lisa was trying to kick him some more, but he held her out of range. She started biting his hand and drew blood.

Walt straightened up and grinned. He grabbed her skimpy dress by its V neck and ripped it off in one smooth motion like he was unveiling a statue. She was naked except for blue panties and white high-heels. Jook moved toward the sofa to get a better view. His hand started rubbing the bulge in his pants.

Walt slapped her a couple of times and opened her split lip even more. Blood ran down her chin and dripped onto her tits.

"She's a veritable hellcat, Nick."

He was sweating buckets as he stood there in his leather clothes, grinning from ear to ear. He slapped her a few more times. She was calming down but she still looked mad as hell. I wondered who got the worst of it when her husband beat her.

"Mrs. Perlont," said Nicky, "since you were willing to do a bargain-type thing, it makes me think you really know something, so I got a deal for you."

Walt grasped her other arm, letting go of the one he'd held her by. It had four red welts where his fingers had been.

"I'll call Walt off if you spill what you know. He's starting to drool now, which means in a few minutes I won't be able to stop him if I wanted to."

She spit a combination of saliva and blood in Nicky's direction. Nicky nodded at Walt.

He ripped off her panties and drew back his fist like he was going to pitch a softball. She realized what he was going to do, twisted her legs tightly together, and screamed. Walt took a step forward for leverage. That put him between Nicky's gat and me. He aimed his huge fist at her crotch and pulled it back again like a pendulum. Lisa closed her eyes.

I took two steps, pounded his head with the studded side of the sap, and pushed him over the coffee table on top of Nicky. I heard a crunch when I'd hit him, so I figured he'd be out for a while. Nicky's gun was pinned under Walt's torso. Their combined weight broke the sofa in two. It collapsed like a folding chair, with them in the middle. I leaned over them and bopped Nicky good. Jook circled around to get me from behind. Lisa jumped on his back, knocked off his sunglasses, and scratched at his eyes.

I whirled and sapped him in the midsection, which caused his wad of gum to fly out of his mouth into my face. He struggled to get his wind back. I closed my fist around the sap and gave him a really well-executed right cross to the temple. His eyes jiggled in their sockets and he crumpled to the floor in a heap.

17

It was a great scene. Nicky was sandwiched between Walt's bulk and the busted sofa; Jook lay in a fetal position on the carpet with his head next to the pink elephant's leg; Lisa leaned against the molding in the kitchen doorway, sweating and bleeding, naked except for her high heels; and me, I was looking over the scene, tossing my sap from hand to hand, and feeling pretty damned Errol Flynnish about the whole thing.

I pried the .45 from under Walt and mentally crossed him off my revenge list. I'd got him good. The crack I heard when I hit him sure sounded like bone to me. I thought I might have fractured his skull. I'd hit Nicky with the unstudded side, so I figured he'd end up with no more than a headache and a bruise. Jook was in the same boat as Nicky.

I brought Lisa into the kitchen and rinsed her face with a damp paper towel. Her lip was cut pretty good, but it didn't need stitches. Both cheeks were reddening from Walt's slaps and there was a little discoloration under one eye. I wiped the blood from her breasts and stomach and sat her down on a chair.

There were some bandages and Mercurochrome in the medicine cabinet in the bathroom. I got them and fixed up Lisa's lip. She hadn't said a word since the fight. She seemed to be getting faint. I carried her into her room and dropped her on the bed. She closed her eyes. I went to the living room.

I stretched them out on their stomachs in a row on the carpet. There was nothing to tie them up with except the cords from two lamps, the toaster, the TV set, and two extension cords. I tied their hands behind them, bound their feet, and bent their knees back to hogtie them. When I finished, I sat in the chair and examined my handiwork. Those boys weren't going anywhere.

I took my shirt off and fanned myself with a magazine. The heat was getting to me. I hadn't had much energy that day to begin with, so after knocking out and tying up three thugs I was spent. I closed my eyes and thought about cool breezes and iced coffee.

I woke up laughing. I had dreamed that Lisa and I were swimming naked off the coast of some tropical isle. It was one of those Technicolor dreams with deep blue water and sky, bright green foliage, and a white beach. We were swimming along, talking and laughing as we went, when Lisa looked back and screamed. I looked and saw Nicky, Walt, and Jook swimming after us. They were sharks. I yelled at Lisa to swim like hell for the beach. We swam as hard as we could, but they were gaining fast. They caught up with us a few yards from shore. We were exhausted. We gave up and turned to meet our fate. The Nicky, Jook, and Walt sharks had turned into big, blue, rubber fish with white bellies. One had a skinny black tie around its snout. Another had a leather cap hooked over its dorsal fin. The third was wearing sunglasses and chewing gum. We towed them to the beach, lined them up on the sand, looked at each other, and burst out laughing.

I was still chuckling as I looked around the room. It was dark outside. The overhead light was on. The air conditioner was humming. Lisa was in the kitchen making cooking sounds. The smell of broiling steak made my stomach rumble.

"What's so funny?" she called from the kitchen.

"Ever see a shark wearing sunglasses?"

"What?"

"Have you ever seen a shark chewing gum and wearing sunglasses?"

"Not recently."

"Then don't ask what's funny, 'cause you wouldn't get the joke."

"You're crazy."

Jook was moaning. Nicky was still out. The side of his face lay in a puddle of saliva. Walt was snoring peacefully. I bent over and felt a big lump under his close-cropped hair. I reconsidered my original diagnosis. If I had really cracked his bean I didn't think he'd be breathing so smoothly. He was more asleep than out cold.

I walked into the kitchen. She was wearing black slacks and a white blouse. Her back was to me as she stirred something on the stove. I came up behind her, snaked my arms around her ribs, and gave her tits a gentle squeeze.

"My, my. You're in a good mood," she said, turning in my arms to face me.

"I guess I am. I don't know why I should be."

I kissed her forehead and stepped back to examine her face. Her lips were blue and swollen. There was an A-1 shiner under her right eye and her cheeks were a little puffy.

"You sure took your lumps today."

"I've had practice."

"I could tell. I've never seen a woman get so angry. I hope you never get that mad at me."

"Me, too."

She went back to stirring. I sat on one of the metal-and-plastic chairs that surrounded a small table under the window.

"But I'm going to take that chance."

"What chance?"

"Of getting you mad."

She pulled the steak out of the broiler. I was hungry and it smelled good.

"On second thought, I think I'll wait till after dinner to get you mad. I'd rather have that steak in my stomach than on my face."

"Suit yourself."

I set the table. We ate steak—medium-rare; how did she know?—green beans and rice. Neither one of us said a word during the meal. She made some drip coffee afterward. I lit a cigarette and sipped. I felt awake and refreshed for the first time in days.

"Lenny, what are we going to do with those awful men in there?"

"That's a real good question. Sooner or later we're gonna have to give them to the cops. We can hit them with breaking and entering, assault with a deadly weapon, assault and battery—the works. We can't let them go, that's for sure. They'd turn around and give us the Blinky treatment."

"So they're just going to stay there in my living room?"

"For now that's about it. I gotta have a talk with a Mr. Birmingham before I know what to do with them and when to do it."

"Who's he?"

"Lisa," I said, ignoring the question, "you've got to answer some questions now. If you want to get mad, go ahead, but it won't make the questions go away."

She put her coffee cup in its saucer, examined a square of linoleum tile, glanced out the window, touched the bandage on her lip, and turned those green peepers on me full force.

"All right," she said, "all right, Perry Mason, fire at will."

"Where's the gun?"

"I don't know."

"Why are Blinky's clothes and stuff all packed?"

Her eyes widened a bit.

"Because you said that you were going to find him and make him go away, so I thought I'd pack his things and send them to wherever he went. I did it because I was alone and nervous and I didn't know what was going on and I wanted something to do to keep me from thinking and worrying."

"Fair enough."

"Anything else?"

"Yeah. The gun doesn't matter at this point because no one's said it was the murder weapon. And I believe what you say about why you packed the boxes. But…"

"Well?"

"Where's the cocaine?"

"Not you too."

She was getting mad. I spoke fast.

"Nicky thought it was an 'interesting-type' thing that Blinky wanted you to meet him. I think it's interesting too. And then it seemed like you were fishing for some kind of deal before Walt started in."

"I don't know why Blinky wanted me to meet him." She was starting to get loud. "I thought maybe he wanted money. And I was just trying to stall that Nicky person. I thought I could fool him and force him to take us out in the open, where we could get help."

I chewed on that for a few seconds. I didn't like the way it tasted.

"Well?" She said it like one of those bitches at Bloomingdale's when they're made to wait for a saleswoman.

"Well nothing. I'm out of questions."

"Good. I didn't like the ones you were asking."

"I didn't like asking them."

We had another cup of coffee. She moved her chair close to mine and put a hand on my thigh. She leaned toward me and rested a chin on my shoulder.

"Are you always so suspicious?" softly, in low tones.

She nibbled on my earlobe.

I put my arm around her and kissed her cheek.

"I think I heard Marlene Dietrich ask that in a movie. I can't remember which one. I think she said it to David Niven or some suave turd like that."

"And what did he say to Marlene?"

"He just kissed her and looked her in the eye and didn't say a word."

"How mysterious of him."

"Yeah."

"I wish you could kiss me now, but this bandage is in the way."

"Let's have a look at your wound."

I peeled off the gauze and the adhesive tape. It was ugly but it had closed perfectly. There probably wouldn't even be a scar. I washed it again in warm, soapy water while she squirmed. I replaced the bandage.

"Well, that was a great meal," I said. "A miracle will now occur. I'll do the dishes."

"Bravo, bravo."

I put all the dishes in the sink and turned on the hot water. As the sink filled up I kept getting pictures of phones in my mind. I was positive that the phone would ring. It took about ten minutes to do the dishes. The phone didn't ring. It was annoying. My premonitions are rarely wrong.

"Lisa, do me a favor? Look up AC-DC's number and find out if they're open tonight."

"Okay."

She went into the living room.

"Lenny?"

"What?"

"They ripped the phone cord out of the wall."

"That explains it."

"What?"

She returned to the kitchen.

"I had a feeling the phone was going to ring. Now I know why it didn't."

"Were you expecting a call?"

"Nope. You were."

"Who?"

"The cops."

"In that case I'm glad the phone's out."

"No, you aren't."

"What do you mean?"

"If they've been trying to get through and find out the phone's out of order, they're going to think that's fishy and come up in person. They said they were going to contact you, didn't they?"

"Yes."

"I'm surprised they haven't been here yet."

"What do we do if they come?"

"Well, we don't want them to find our friends—not yet. The last thing we need is them saying how they saw us next to a body that was supposed to be on the other side of town. We just won't be here when they come. In fact, you're going to be a good citizen and go down there yourself and offer to answer questions."

"Where are you going to be?"

"AC-DC's, if it's open." I put my hands on her shoulders. "We gotta be careful. We got to do this right or we could end up in jail, or worse. Y'know what I mean?"

She nodded solemnly.

"Put on some makeup. If they ask about your face, tell 'em you fell down or something. Try and make it look like you had an accident, not a beating."

"I'll try."

"What else? Oh, yeah. If they ask about the phone,

say that you were out—I don't know—walking in the park or something, trying to relax and that's why you didn't know your phone was out."

She shuffled off to her room. I went to the living room. Jook and Nicky were on their sides, trying to untie each other. Walt was still out to lunch.

"Hi, boys," I said. "How's it comin'? It's a bitch to untie wire, ain't it?"

"Fuck you, you cock suckin' piece of …"

"Shut up, shithead," Nicky said. "Can we deal, Hornblower?"

"Nope. Me and the lady are going out for a while. I want you fellas to relax while we're gone."

"At least let me take a leak," said Nicky.

"In your pants, my friend, in your pants."

"Y'know, if you don't let us go you're a dead man. You know that."

"I figure if I let you go I'm a dead man anyway, so you stay."

I grabbed the cord that connected Nicky's hands and feet and pulled him behind the broken sofa. I put Jook in the kitchen and closed the door to prevent further group efforts at knot untying. Three dish towels made adequate gags.

Lisa came in. She'd lipsticked her blue lips red, camouflaged the shiner with powder, and had somehow turned her reddened cheeks into ones that appeared to be a little over-rouged.

"Pretty damn good and damn pretty," I said.

"You have such a way with words."

"I do a lot of crossword puzzles."

"Funny, you don't seem the type."

"I'm full of surprises."

"I'll bet you are." She laughed like it was an inside joke.

"You ready for the police?"

"After what I've been through today, I'm ready for anything."

"Call down and see if José's there."

She walked to the intercom by the front door and buzzed. José answered.

"What do you want me to tell him?"

"Just say you wanted to see if he was back."

She did.

"Is there another way out of this building?" I asked.

"Yes. Take the elevator to the basement, go past the washing machines, and up the stairs. You can't miss it. There's a door opening onto Broadway."

"Okay. Meet me at the car."

I put the gun in my belt and pulled my shirttails out to cover it. It was heavy and cold against my skin. That, together with the sap in my pocket, forced me to tighten my belt a notch to hold my pants up.

Lisa's instructions were accurate. I saw her coming around the corner as I stepped onto the sidewalk. She was walking fast.

"Lenny, a police car pulled up to the building just now."

"I wonder what took them so long. Okay, get down there right away. I'll take a cab to the club. Go there when you're through at the station. Is there an all-night coffee shop around here?"

"Yes, on Eightieth and Broadway."

"If I'm not at the club, go there. If I'm not there, wait for me. Don't go back to your place alone."

"Don't worry about that."

"All right. See you later."

"Kiss me, Lenny."

"It'll hurt your lip."

"I don't mind."

I put my arms around her waist and kissed the side of her mouth. The day before I'd written her off as unattainable and then, boom, there I was kissing her cut lip. There really is something somewhere that waits for you to decide that a thing is impossible and then it gives it to you whether you want it or not. I really believe that.

"Did it hurt?"

"Yeah, but it's a nice pain."

I hailed a cab. The driver couldn't speak English. I asked him if he knew where the Bowery was. He nodded, smiled, and headed uptown. I yelled at him to turn around. He nodded and smiled and make a "U" that threw me across the seat. He had a hard time with the difference between left and right, so I had to lean over the seat and give him hand signals. I didn't tip him when we got to AC-DC's. He understood that perfectly and took off as I was closing the door, almost taking my hand with him.

The club was open. I recognized a few of the people hanging around the entrance. Dora wasn't at her post. In her place was a pleasant-looking girl with curly brown hair and big dark eyes.

"Where's Dora?" I asked her.

"She's off tonight. She might be in later. Can I give her a message?"

"No thanks. Who's playing tonight?"

"The Hairdos and The Snappy Comebacks."

"Is Peter Birmingham here?"

"Yeah. He just walked in."

I paid the cover and went to the bar. Artie was standing in the shadows by the cigarette machine. I didn't see Birmingham or Stu.

It was easily as crowded as the night before and none the worse for the blackout. I ordered Scotch and leaned against the bar. Some lugs were moving equipment around on the stage. The jukebox played constantly. I never noticed anyone putting money into it, but it never stopped.

I spotted Birmingham sitting by the wall at the table I'd sat at the night before. Alone, he was drumming his fingers on the table and looking around. I wondered if he was waiting for Nick and friends.

I made my way to his table and sat across from him. He seemed about as happy to see me as a fly looking at a No-Pest Strip.

"Seen Nicky tonight?" I asked.

"No." He spit it out without looking at me.

"You expect to see him?"

"Look, buster, I don't know what your game is"—he looked at my chest as he spoke—"but I'm gonna know it soon enough. Right now I'm not interested in talking to you, so why don't you get out of my sight?"

He had a Brooklyn accent that made "why" sound like "woy." It reminded me of the way Roxanne used to speak. It annoyed me then too.

"It's a shame about Blinky, isn't it?"

He looked up sharply. The bags under his eyes, his jowls, and his fleshy lips quivered with the movement.

I continued. "I wonder if he spoke to anyone before he … left."

"You ought to know."

"Seems like a lot of people feel that way. I'll let you in on a secret. I don't know a goddamn thing. You believe that?"

"I believe you're in big trouble and you don't know what to do about it and you're fishing for information."

He was more or less right. For the first time I felt like I was dealing with someone with real brains.

"I got news for you," I said. "We're both in trouble."

He tilted his head to the side and focused on my forehead.

"Are you threatening me?"

"No."

"Then what's your point?"

"There are some people who are bothering me. They bothered me today. I want to work out a way so they don't bother me anymore."

"What do you have in mind?"

"I was going to let you make a suggestion."

"What if I don't want to."

"That's when I threaten you."

"With what?"

"I'd rather avoid it."

I looked away as if something had caught my attention. I was giving him time to think about a deal. He drummed on the table and followed my line of vision as if his attention was attracted by the same thing mine was. I was a novice at this kind of haggling. It was his strong suit. I not only needed a trump card, I needed to know when to play it.

I looked at him.

"You got a suggestion for me?"

"No."

"Okay, pal."

A band walked onstage. The bass drum had "Snappy Comebacks" lettered on it. I took a deep breath.

"I hear you and your band are going to South America soon."

"Come to the point, prick."

"They got a lot of cocaine down there. What they don't have is an interest in rock music. Makes me wonder why you're going. Know what I mean?"

"You're playing out of your league, buster."

"Well, why don't you put me on waivers, call off your

dogs, and that'll be that."

The band's first song cut off our conversation. He kept looking at my chest and that made me nervous. I signaled to him that I was going to get a drink. Stu came into the club as I reached the bar.

He made a beeline for Birmingham's table. I ordered another Scotch and turned to face them. Artie came, sat next to Birmingham, and pointed at me. Stu followed the line of his finger, saw me, and did a double take that Lou Costello would have been proud of.

I smiled at them and waved.

Something was going on in front of the stage. The singer, a black-haired, sallow rail who looked and dressed like one of the junkies who hang around the Port Authority Bus Terminal, had been singing a song that, as near as I could tell, had something to do with wanting to be somebody's dog. In the moments when he wasn't singing, he was spraying the people sitting in the first few rows of tables with hefty gobs of spit. A short, beefy guy wearing a T-shirt that said "Property of Hofstra University Athletic Department" on the back stood and heaved a beer bottle at him. Two guys wearing "Snappy Comebacks" T-shirts who had set up the equipment emerged from the passageway at the left of the stage. They went over to Hofstra and started poking fingers into his chest. He shoved one of them. They shoved him. He fell over his chair and came up holding the chair over his head. The people at the surrounding tables stood and backed away. He didn't look like he had the balls to swing the chair, and they didn't look like they had the balls to provoke him. Neither side wanted to back down.

The "dog" song ended. The singer, in a voice that kept breaking like a fifteen-year-old's, said, "Will someone tell that fuckin' jerk that he's a fuckin' jerk?"

He punctuated that with another gob that struck Hofstra in the ear. He let out a nice college yell and heaved the chair at the singer. I was impressed by the graceful leap that saved his legs from being mashed by the chair. Unfortunately, he landed on the edge of the metal disc that supported the mike stand. His ankle turned, pitching him forward off the stage and into the laps of a pair of girls wearing matching, ripped, red T-shirts and black pegged pants. Hofstra dove between the girls and started beating the living shit out of the singer. The two equipment guys dove on top of the heap and started beating the living shit out of Hofstra. One of the girls managed to extricate herself and was clawing away at anyone within reach. Her T-shirt got ripped a little more so that her left breast hung neatly out of a hole that looked like the ass flap on a baby's pajamas.

The three other band members were leaning over the edge of the stage, laughing and shouting encouragement to Hofstra. They seemed to enjoy seeing their lead singer at the bottom of the pile.

The crowd had pressed back, giving the melee room. They didn't seem to mind the fight. I supposed it was part of the show. A couple of guys were shaking beer bottles and spraying the combatants.

Artie appeared and calmly flung each person in a different direction until he grabbed the singer and lifted him to his feet by his shirt collar. The guy was bleeding from the nose and mouth. The band helped him onstage and gave him something to drink.

A big fellow wearing a yellow hardhat came over with a couple of bartenders and hustled all the principals toward the door. One of the equipment guys, as he was pushed past me, said, "But I work for the band, man. I work for the band."

"Shut up," Hardhat said calmly.

The singer disappeared into the back for a few seconds and then returned holding a bloodstained handkerchief to his face. The crowd cheered. The band started playing an instrumental as he tipped his head back, waiting for his nose to stop bleeding. He banged a tambourine against his thigh with his free hand. They played for maybe two minutes when he motioned them to stop. He threw the reddened hankie to the crowd and screamed into the microphone.

"You're a bunch of blockheads. My bar mitzvah was more exciting than this."

That earned him another cheer. He started talking with a jive black accent.

"Now we gonna do our disco number. 'S called 'Stand Up and Sit Down!'"

His nose started bleeding again after a few bars and he let the blood flow. No one seemed to think it gory or tasteless. I thought it was disgusting, but I couldn't take my eyes off him.

A guy standing next to me at the bar said, "Who's he think he is? Iggy? What an asshole."

The lyrics of the song consisted entirely of "Stand up and sit down." Toward the end the singer tried to get everyone to get up when he said "Stand up" and then sit with "Sit down." No one moved. When the song ended he screamed that the audience was made up of "wimps." That got him another round of applause. There was some weird psychology going on that I didn't understand. The more rude, arrogant, and condescending that jerk was, the more they liked him. Even if they didn't respond to the music, they ate up his insults and applauded his grossness. I felt old. I just didn't understand it.

Birmingham tapped me on the shoulder. I turned

to face him. I'd never seen him upright before. He was a little shorter than me, with drooping shoulders and a little potbelly. If anyone was a wimp, he was.

"I gotta go now." He looked at my throat. He never once looked me in the eye. "I'm thinking about what you said. Come up to my office tomorrow—180 West Fifty-eighth Street, tenth floor, American Management Associates. I'll be there from noon till five."

I nodded.

He and Stu huddled with Artie at the far end of the bar for a couple of minutes. They left. I caught Artie's eye and he pretended to look past me.

I decided not to wait for Lisa. I didn't want to be seen there with her anyway. I left and hailed a cab. This time I got one of those Jewish guys who'd been hacking for forty years and know every street in all five boroughs. I gave him the address of the coffee shop and settled back into the seat. He asked me if I'd "heard the one about ..." and proceeded to reel off one-liners all the way to Eightieth Street.

18

"So this Jewish kid says to his father, 'Papa, vat's a vacuum?'

"And the father says, 'Veil, son, a vacuum's a void.'

"And the kid says, 'I know it's a void, Papa, but vat's de void mean?'"

He honked twice to punctuate the joke. We got to Eightieth and Broadway before he could start another.

The coffee shop wasn't a coffee shop at all. The sign read: "THE LATIN MANDARIN." Underneath that, printed on the window, was: "CHINESE-SPANISH CUISINE—OPEN 24 HOURS."

I walked in trying to imagine what Chinese-Spanish food tasted like. A nervous Chink led me to a small booth in the back. The menu had two columns on each side. On the far left were the Chinese dishes listed in English. Next to that they were listed in Spanish. The next column had the Spanish food in English. The righthand one was Spanish-Spanish. On the back were two more columns in Chinese. Underneath the Chinese it said: "Latin Mandarin Deluxe—Hamburger. French Fries. Salad."

It was about eleven-thirty. Some people were sitting at the counter in the front. A few of the booths near me were occupied. On the wall to my right was a mural depicting an aerial view of a bunch of bulls chasing people down a narrow street. Opposite, a large grid of bamboo staves adorned with exotic plastic fronds and flowers hung from a chain. The waiters were Oriental. The busboys were Puerto Rican. The cashier was a fat, blue-haired white lady in a puke-green, sleeveless dress. All the customers except me were black. All we needed was an Apache and we could form our own U.N.

The nervous waiter came over to take my order. He kept glancing down at my shirt. I asked for shrimp fried rice. He wrote it down and backed away, bowing as he went and bumping into chairs. I looked down. The butt of the automatic extended out between my shirttails. All I needed was for him to go get some cop.

I saw him chirping in Chinese at one of the younger guys over by the counter. It looked like they were planning strategy in case I tried to rob the place.

The younger guy brought the food. I smiled and tried to look as unthreatening as possible. I sat back so he could look for the gun that I'd shoved out of sight. He looked and turned away with a smirk on his face. He went over to his nervous chum and spat out three harsh syllables in a sarcastic tone. "You're nuts" sounds the same in any language.

I wasn't hungry but I think better when I eat. I thought about Birmingham first. He scared me. He was smart. He'd said three things at the club that were right on the button: I wasn't sure what to do; I was fishing for info; I was playing out of my league. I tried to remember what Nicky had said about him, something about how he'd sell you a five-dollar bill for seven-fifty and then steal it back. I hadn't taken it seriously then because Nicky'd looked like such a doofo, but I took it seriously now, very seriously.

The way I saw it was that Birmingham was the brains and the money man for the organization. Nicky was in charge of operations. Birmingham probably procured the drugs and gave them to Nicky on consignment, so when three pounds of coke get stolen by one of Nicky's boys, Nicky's in big trouble with Birmingham. He's got to get the stuff back or make good on it—or else.

I didn't think Birmingham was involved with the hijacking. That was probably Nicky's own racket although, likely as not, Nutty Nicky's was collateral for the drugs. I wondered if Nicky had told Birmingham that six more pounds were missing. If I was right about the way they operated, Nicky would be desperate as hell to recover the dope—maybe desperate enough to kill Blinky or to have him killed.

There was a problem with that theory though. It wouldn't serve Nicky's purpose to bump off Twitchface before he knew where the stuff was, and he obviously didn't. It was time for a new list of facts. I ordered coffee, a paper napkin, and got out the BIC Click. I lit a cigarette.

1. Blinky was dead, shot through the heart, his pin ripped from his nose.

2. Suspects: Birmingham, Nicky, Walt, Stu, Jook, Artie, Dora, and Lisa.

3. Whoever killed him had my wallet.

4. Someone, not necessarily the killer, moved the body.

5. I'd told Blinky that all the people he wanted most to avoid were going to be at the club that night, and yet he went there anyway. Why?

I couldn't think of any other facts. Everything else was conjecture. I tapped the pen against my teeth and watched the fat cashier examine her reflection in the window. My conversation after dinner with Lisa floated through my mind. I thought about the only time I'd seen Blinky and her together. Something had clicked in my head then. I'd been surprised at the way he'd called her "Lisa" instead of "Mom." It wouldn't have been odd if I'd known then that he was her stepson. It was the way he'd said it that was odd. I didn't know why. It just was.

I remembered another fact.

6. The pistol was gone from the drawer.

It wasn't really relevant. I had no way of knowing what type of gun did the blasting. For all I knew the one tucked against my hip was the murder weapon. I looked up and let out a low whistle. If I got caught by the police with the .45 in my pants and it turned out to be the murder gun, I'd be on a bus to Attica in less time than it'd take to say, "You guys are making a big mistake." I decided to ditch the gun in a safe place at the earliest opportunity.

I ordered another cup of coffee. The waiter brought a couple of fortune cookies with it. The first one said:

Decisive action is the way
To keep your troubles all at bay.

That one didn't thrill me too much. I crumbled the other cookie:

There is a woman in your life
Who gives you love and brings you strife.

Lisa walked through the door, looked around, saw me, and smiled. I rolled the slip of paper into a tight ball and swallowed it with a gulp of coffee.

"You hungry?" I said as she sat down.

"No, but I would like some coffee." She saw me fold up my napkin of facts. "What's that?"

"Nothing. How'd it go at the station house?"

"Well, they were very nice. They had me look at pictures to see if I could recognize you, and they asked me all about Blinky's friends and so forth. And that was about all."

"Did they mention anything about me?"

"Only that they were watching your place and that it was just a matter of time till they got you."

"Great. Looks like I'll have to wear these clothes till this thing is over."

I ordered coffee for her. The nervous waiter seemed a bit more at ease now that I had a respectable looking lady with me.

"Did you see the man you wanted to talk with?" she asked.

"Yeah. He wasn't real happy to see me. We didn't get a chance to really talk. I'm gonna see him tomorrow."

"Does he have something to do with those men in the apartment?"

"Yeah."

She waited for an explanation. I smiled and sipped coffee.

"You don't want me to ask questions, do you? You don't trust me."

"I just don't want to talk about what I'm not sure of. Finish your coffee and let's go see how the Happiness Boys are doing."

We paid and walked the two blocks to her place. José wasn't at the door.

"I don't like this," I said under my breath. "What time does José get off work?"

"Not till two or so, and then another man comes."

The lobby was too quiet. I had a bad feeling about something.

"Let's take the stairs," I said.

"Why?"

"I need the exercise, and besides, if anyone is waiting to say hello to us, they'll be watching the elevator."

José was propped against the wall on the landing one level above the basement. Lisa started down.

"Forget him. We don't want to be the ones to find him. He'll wake up soon enough."

I got the .45 and took off the safety. On the fifth floor I glanced through the small square window and saw a quiet, empty hall.

"Wait here," I whispered.

"Like hell I will."

"Well, then stay behind me."

"Okay, okay."

I walked to 5-D. The lock had been kicked in. The door was about halfway open, giving me a view of the broken sofa, the elephants, and the empty expanse of carpet where I'd left the cruds. I pushed the door all the way to the inside wall and listened.

"Now you wait here, goddammit."

"All right, all right."

"If anything happens, run like hell and get the cops."

I walked in, looked in the kitchen, the bedrooms and the bathroom. Every drawer in every room was open and in disarray. The cupboards in the kitchen looked like the aftermath of a block party. The cushions on the sofa and the pillows and mattresses in the bedroom had been slit. The boxes in Blinky's room were emptied onto the floor. They'd even torn the back off the TV set. A hurricane had nothing on them.

"Come on in. The rats have scuttled the ship."

She stepped in on tiptoes, as if someone might still be there to hear her.

"I can't believe they managed to untie themselves," she said, standing in the center of the living room surveying the rubble.

"They didn't."

"Then what …"

"They probably left word where they were going to be, and when they didn't come back, their friends came for them."

She plopped down on the chair and started laughing.

"What's so funny?"

"I was just thinking last week that I ought to do some redecorating."

"Well, you're going to have to now."

I brought one of the kitchen chairs into the living room and sat.

"It must of taken them hours," she said.

"Nope, I don't think so. There were at least four of them, maybe five. I bet they could have done it in fifteen minutes. What smells?"

I looked around and saw two dark patches on the

brown carpet.

"I guess they did do it in their pants."

"Yuck. Let's get out of here."

"Good idea. How much cash do you have?"

"Twenty dollars or so. Why?"

"Got any credit cards?"

"American Express."

"Good. Let's find a hotel. We shouldn't stay here any longer than we have to. They probably went from here to the club to find me. They'll be back."

"Lenny, what about José?"

"What about him?"

"He's going to call the police when he comes to."

"Oh, yeah. I hadn't thought of that. It doesn't matter, I guess. They'll just think it was burglars."

"But if they see it was my apartment that was broken into, won't they wonder why I didn't report it? And won't they think it's strange that my place gets burglarized a day after …"

"Well, there's nothing we can do about it. With any luck we'll be able to give the whole crew over to the cops before the cops find us. I won't feel safe till all those guys are put away."

"What kind of luck did you have in mind?"

"I haven't the slightest idea."

"That's encouraging."

"Yeah. Where shall we spend the night?"

"I don't know. I've never slept in a hotel in New York. Have you?"

"Nope."

"Wait. I know. When my parents visited once they stayed at someplace on Twentieth or Twenty-first and Lexington. Oh, what was it called?"

"That's near Gramercy Park."

"That's it."

"What's it?"

"That's the name of the hotel."

"Okay. The Gramercy Park Hotel it is."

Lisa threw some clothes in a bag while I tried to make the door look like it hadn't been forced. We took the elevator down and went out onto the street. The Datsun was parked near The Latin Mandarin. It was my fourth trip downtown that day.

The hotel was across the street from the park. We pushed through the revolving door, went to the long oaken desk, and registered as Mr. and Mrs. Horn. Our room was on the sixth floor. It looked out onto Lexington Avenue. Yellow and white wallpaper, yellow bedspreads, and a yellow and brown carpet—bright and cheery.

I called room service and ordered sandwiches, beer, and cigarettes. I flopped on the bed and stared at the light fixture on the ceiling, letting my eyes go out of focus. Lisa sat in a chair by the window and read a magazine she'd bought downstairs. Room service arrived. I drank both beers and she nibbled on one of the sandwiches.

I tried to form some sort of plan for my meeting with Birmingham. The vague one I'd decided on was scotched because Nicky and friends had gotten away. I figured as a last resort I could trade the coke I had stashed at the post office for some kind of guarantee that they'd leave me alone. That, however, didn't solve my problem with the cops. The solution to that was to hand them a killer along with some nice solid evidence.

Lisa looked up from her magazine.

"I don't believe it."

"What?"

"That I'm here in this hotel room with you, that I can't go home, that I'm mixed up in this incredible mess."

She smiled and shook her head. I patted the bed. She came over and stretched out next to me, slipping her hand inside my shirt to play with my chest hair. I ran my fingers through her dark straight hair and brushed the bangs away from her forehead. She unbuttoned my shirt and started planting moist smooches on my chest.

"Why is it," she said between kisses, "that you don't trust me? You must have a reason."

"Who said that I don't trust you?"

"God. Men are so obvious."

"What's that supposed to mean?"

"Every time I ask you a question about what's going on you either ignore it or change the subject or give me double talk. Of course, you never said, 'I don't trust you,' but you make it obvious."

I didn't want to answer her. I didn't want to tell her that I didn't believe she really liked me, that I thought she was playing the stereotyped role of the seductive young beauty out to use, and therefore make a fool of, the middle-aged lonely man, that I thought she was doing it because she had something to hide. But, most of all, I didn't want to tell her that I didn't care if she was using me. I felt that if I said it out loud, it would all end. I didn't want it to end, no matter how phony and deluding it was.

"It's not that I don't trust you." I focused on the light fixture again. "It's just that I'm not sure about the way things stand."

"Don't play word games. That means the same thing."

"No it doesn't."

"What do I have to do?" She started getting loud. "I could have turned you in to the police any number of

times. I've made love to you. I gave you money, I'm
even paying for this goddamn room."

"Thank you."

"Fuck you," she yelled.

"Well, what the hell is it you want me to say?" I
yelled back. I didn't feel like yelling, but the line called
for it.

She sat up and slapped my stomach.

"I want to know just what it is you think I've done."

She stood and started walking around the room,
crying.

"My stepson is dead. I've been beaten black and
blue. My home is destroyed." She paused, then
whispered, "Oh, my god."

"What?"

"I could be killed. You said so yourself. I didn't really
think about it but … I just realized it. Jesus."

She let out a sound that was halfway between a
laugh and a sob. I sat up and took her arm, pulling
her onto my lap. She put her arms around my neck
and wept. She felt small as I held her, her body heaving
rhythmically with her sobs. My chest tightened. I
wanted to sit on her goddamn lap and bawl. I couldn't.
I got that feeling in the back of my throat and my
eyes started to water, but I just couldn't. I still didn't
believe her.

She raised her head and looked into my eyes, her
green ones rimmed with red and overflowing with
liquid. Her mouth was open and her lips quivered.
Her nostrils flared with each hesitant inhalation. All
the makeup she'd put on was mixing together in the
paths her tears were taking down her cheeks. I began
to sway back and forth. The crying passed. We sat,
holding each other tightly.

She looked up at me again and sniffled.

"Please help me."

"To do what?"

"Just don't desert me."

She put on that earnest look again, only this time it was mixed with the pathetic one. I cursed myself for not being able to accept it as real; the only times I'd ever seen that look was in movies. It was the same one Shirley Temple used in *Wee Willie Winkie* when she begged the caliph not to shoot the gruff-but-kindly old colonel.

"I've never been mixed up in anything like this," she continued, "and I don't know which way to turn and you've helped me all along and you're the only one I can rely on and now that I've fallen ... now that I, we are ... together like this ... I just wouldn't know what to do if you ..."

"Please shut up," I said, smiling. I felt like her dad. "I know what you're trying to say. I need you too. I started out in this thing with a certain goal in mind, and now, well, I guess it's changed. You made it change. Let's not talk this way anymore, okay? I'm no good at it. Anyway, everything I say sounds like it's lifted from 'As the World Turns.'"

"I thought you were good with words."

"And I thought you were a hellcat."

"You better believe I am," she said as she wiped her eyes with the hem of the bedspread. "Just get me mad and I'll show you who's a hellcat."

"Did you ever get real mad at Blinky?"

"Of course. One time he tried to feel me up and I cut his arm with a knife. I told him if he ever ..."

She sat up straight and blinked. Her eyes narrowed, her head tilted, and her left fist shot out at my nose. I caught her wrist and bent her arm behind her, turning her around. I pulled her down on the bed and got her in a good full nelson till her tantrum passed.

"You never let up," she snarled, "do you?"

"And you've got the sense of humor of a bear I once saw at the Central Park zoo."

I released my hold and lay on my back on the bed. She moved next to me and draped an arm across my chest.

"What bear? What are you talking about?"

"One day I was at the zoo and there was this big, brown bear lying in a pool of water. He was real calm. He looked like he didn't have a care in the world. Then this black guy, one of the guys who worked there, came around with a pail of meat and he starts teasing the bear. He was sayin' stuff like, 'C'mon outta there, you big ole homo bear. Come and get your raw meat, you ole buttfucker.' The bear didn't move. He just lay there with his head and front paws out of the water and made like the last thing in the world that would bother him was that black zookeeper. The guy kept at him. 'You the ugliest bear I ever saw. Why don't you go ugly up somebody else's zoo? I got half a mind to give your meat to some good-lookin' bear. Ugly bear like you don't deserve no food.'"

My imitation of the zookeeper was either great or terrible, because Lisa was laughing pretty hard.

"I thought it was pretty funny, the way the bear was ignoring him and what he was saying. A bunch of people gathered around, listening to the guy tease the bear, and laughing. The guy turned a little to look at the crowd. That fuckin' bear let out a roar and was out of the water and at the bars swiping his claws at the guy before he realized what was going on. He missed him by a hair. The keeper was so scared he just threw the meat through the bars and took off. The bear kept roaring at him until he was out of sight."

"And I remind you of that bear?"

"Yeah. The two of you got no sense of humor."

"Well," she said, unbuckling my belt and pulling down the zipper, "let's pretend you're the keeper and I'm the bear."

"I'll have to declaw you first."

"No, I don't think so."

She ran a fingernail along the underside of my cock. I shuddered.

19

I woke up at ten-thirty the next morning. I had commandeered the sheet during the night, so Lisa was uncovered when I looked at her. She was lying on her side, her back arched, her flat, white stomach inviting my hand. Her eyes fluttered and closed at my touch. She mumbled and turned over.

I went into the bathroom and took a shower. She was still asleep when I came out. I opened the window and inhaled some clear, warm air. It was the kind of New York City summer day that you get only once or twice a year. The sky was a shade of blue so pure and deep that it looked out of place. The buildings seemed in sharper focus. Their windows reflecting the sunlight seemed somehow cleaner, as if the breeze from the river had wiped away the constant greasy film. I could smell the soil and trees from the park. It was the kind of day that commands you to accomplish something.

I tried to wake up Lisa, but she wanted to sleep some more. I got dressed, went down to the lobby, and bought copies of the *Times*, the *Post*, and the *News*. The cool wind that hit me as I stepped outside reminded me that I'd better get something done—and done well. I walked to Third Avenue, found a coffee shop, and settled down to a glass of milk, a cup of coffee, and the newspapers.

The *News* and *Post* had nothing about Blinky. I turned to the local news page of the *Times*, right next to the obits, and checked the Metropolitan Briefs. It was there, a few lines in the Police Blotter section:

> The body of Gerald Perlont, 17, 132 West Eighty-second Street, was found in an empty lot on Tenth Avenue between Fifteenth and Sixteenth streets. He had been shot once; no apparent motive.

I finished the coffee and went for a walk up Third. Something was bothering me. Why the hell did Blinky go to AC's that night? It must have been important or he wouldn't have taken such a risk. And then, why call Lisa to meet him there? Maybe there were no reasons. The kid was crazy. Maybe he didn't know what he was doing.

The wind was whipping around much harder at Thirty-fourth Street. When I got to Forty-second, it was blowing enough to make me lean into it. A bunch of kids on the corner wearing "Jews for Jesus" T-shirts were scurrying after hundreds of little yellow pamphlets that the wind was kicking around the street. I thought there was something symbolic or ironic about that, but I had neither the energy nor the inclination to figure it out. I trapped one of the pamphlets under my shoe. It said: "Are you a schlemiel or a schlimazel?"

I reached Fiftieth, went over to Park, and headed back downtown. It was around noontime. Birmingham had said any time between noon and five.

He and Stu had left AC-DC's together the previous night. I had to assume that Stu had gone uptown alone. If Stu had gone alone, they might have decided not to tell Birmingham what happened for fear of his wrath at bungling the job, not to mention plain old embarrassment. Also, I didn't think Birmingham would be a party to assaulting José or breaking and entering, at least not in person. The little matter of an additional six pounds of missing coke would, if Birmingham had known about it, have caused him to not let me out of his sight. I decided to proceed on the assumption that Nicky and friends were keeping Birmingham in the dark about that, which was fine with me. An enemy divided is almost an ally.

Staying with the enemy divided assumption, I figured it was more or less safe to go to Birmingham's office. I doubted if Nicky would be hanging around unless he had been in touch with Birmingham and found out I was going to be there sometime that day. I wasn't even too worried about that. I could tell Birmingham about the six pounds, which would take the heat off of me and put it on Nicky. What really worried me was the possibility that Birmingham had some neat scheme that I would jump into head first.

I walked back to the hotel and found Lisa awake, dressed, and brushing her hair.

"Where'd you go off to?"

"For a walk. It's a beautiful day."

"What's on the agenda today?"

"I've got to speak to someone uptown. I should be back by late afternoon. What are you going to do?"

"I don't know. Nothing, I suppose."

"You don't work, do you?"

"No."

"How do you support yourself?"

"Well, if you must know, Roger, Blinky's father, left Blinky quite a large sum of money when he died. Since I became his legal guardian, I have control of that money until Blinky turns twenty-one. I guess it's obvious that I took in Blinky out of more than just a sense of responsibility."

"Yeah, it's obvious. Tell me something, is there a lot left?"

"A lot of what?"

"Of Blinky's inheritance."

"We haven't even touched the principal. I'm not even sure how much that is. We've been living off the interest and dividends, and that's added up to between twenty and twenty-five thousand a year."

I whistled.

"Here's a question you're gonna love," I said. "Who gets the loot now?"

"I guess I do."

She said it nice and clear without so much as a downward glance of humility.

"The cops know that?"

"Yes."

"It's a good thing I'm the number one suspect, isn't it?"

"What do you mean by that?"

"Well"—I paused, wondering if I should be vague or direct; I decided on direct—"'cause if I wasn't, you would be. It's a hell of a motive."

"I suppose it is."

I thought she'd get mad, but she didn't. Every other time I had implied that she was involved in something shady she had given me what-for.

"Well?" she said.

"Well what?"

"I'm waiting for Perry Mason to fire at will."

I shrugged.

"I'm going to let it sink in. Now, if you'll forgive me for changing the subject, did you happen to bring Junior's address book with you?"

"No."

"Well, then do me a favor. Go up to your place at some point today and get it. I don't think there's any danger now. And besides, you could ask José about last night if he's there. Give him the impression your place wasn't broken into. Come to think of it, find out if it was one or two men who conked him. That would be a big help."

"I suppose it would be useless to ask why it would be a big help and why you want the address book."

"Yeah." I stuffed the .45 in my pants.

"You're something else, you know that?" She put her hands on her hips. "You make me feel like I'm two different people. Sometimes I feel like a love-struck girl who's having an affair with an older man. And then you make me feel like some scheming Mata Hari who's taking advantage of you in some weird way."

"So?" I said, opening the door to leave.

"So, which is it?"

"Both."

I shut the door behind me fast. The hairbrush must have broken as it hit because I heard two distinct clatters on the floor.

I walked over to Twenty-fourth and Madison and caught a bus up to Fifty-eighth Street. Number 180 was between Sixth and Seventh avenues. It was a relatively small building. A glance at the directory in the lobby showed a lot of M.D.'s, D.D.S.'s, and Inc.'s. I told the elevator operator, "Ten, please." It was one-fifteen.

The double door opposite the elevator said, "10-C—AMERICAN MANAGEMENT ASSOCIATES." I walked in. A pretty black secretary with straight black hair or wig sat behind a desk to my right. The place was a big rectangle, partitioned into sections by ridged strips of opaque glass. I could see four doors down the corridor that the sections formed and it looked like there were more small offices branching off to the left.

"Can I help you?" She had a sweet, unblack voice.

"I want to see Peter Birmingham."

"Do you have an appointment?"

"Sort of. He said to come any time between noon and five."

"Your name?"

"Hornblower. Leonard Hornblower."

"Mr. Hornblower, Mr. Birmingham did not leave word that he was expecting you, but if you'll have a seat"—she nodded toward an uninviting orange vinyl couch—"I'll tell him you're here."

"Right." I sat.

Before she could pick up the phone, four dark-haired, sneakered young guys and one blonde, tightly trousered girl marched in.

"I'm sorry," she said, half-standing, her right arm outstretched as if that could stop them. "I'll have to tell Mr. Birmingham you're here before you can go in."

"Like hell," said one of the guys.

They walked single file down the corridor and opened the farthest door on the right, the corner office. The secretary plopped down into her chair and mumbled something that sounded like "Jive-ass honkies."

I was about to remind her to tell Birmingham I was there when the shouting started. I couldn't distinguish the male voices, except that one was British and didn't do much of the yelling. Birmingham's thick Brooklynese made him identifiable.

"Goddammit. We been touring the fuckin' world for nearly two years now. We got hit songs on three fuckin' continents, gold records, lots of press, and not a fuckin' penny to show for it."

"Wait a minute. Now just wait a minute." It was Birmingham. "You each get a grand a month."

"A grand a month? We could pull twice that on the Jersey Shore circuit playin' top-forty shit. I see the trades. I look at the goddamn numbers. Where's the fuckin' bread, man?"

"Look, you assholes, you had a huge debt to pay when we switched labels. Plus we had to pay off that producer, not to mention what you owe me. It takes time."

"Time?" The girl's voice. "Time?" She loaded the word with more sarcasm than it could take. "In all the *time* we been touring and all the *time* our records have been selling, we've grossed three times that goddamn debt. We wanna see the books. We wanna see receipts. You gotta prove it, man."

"You been talkin' to some lawyer?"

Another voice: "You're fuckin' right we been talkin' to a lawyer. You better come up with some ... some ..."

"Audited books," supplied Britain.

"Yeah—audited books, or you're gonna be talkin' to a lawyer too."

"Look." Birmingham was trying to calm his tone. "After the South American tour I'll show you all the books you ..."

"Uh-uh. Nope. No way. We want 'em *before* the tour—or we don't go."

"Now wait just a minute, prick." He picked up

volume again. "I made deals; everything's arranged. You're going and there's nothing to say about it."

"Like hell, fuckhead." It was the girl again, and she was louder than him. "We aren't so fuckin' stupid. We know you got more riding on this trip than just promoting the band. You wanna make shady coke deals in Bolivia? Go right ahead. It's none of our business, and more power to you. But to have us go down there, where no one's ever heard of us, and use our energy and hard work to cover your fuckin' lowlife schemes —forget it."

"You watch your mouth, bitch."

"You watch who you call bitch."

"Peter," said Britain, loud but calm, "listen, mate, we want more money. We know it's there. You've been stringing us along with this debt and that debt for too long. The end of it is that you either have to give us more money or prove why you can't. We decided to use this tour as a lever to force you to do it. We can do that, y'know. We're a corporation and can act as one entity. In addition, we have been informed that there are clauses in the contract ..."

"Don't start talkin' contract at me. None of you knows anything about it."

The first voice started in again.

"That's another thing. We want a new contract. We want one that guarantees a certain amount of record promotion in the States."

"That's between you and Butterfly Records."

"Then do it, dammit. You talk to the fuckin' label. Are you working for us or against us? You're the one who's supposed to take care of that shit. It says so in the damned contract."

"Wait a minute. Let me get this straight. You want more money. You want to see the books. You want a new contract. Is that right? You want all of that or you don't go on tour."

"That's part of it. We wanna know about the royalties, our publishing company, we want more promotion in the States, and we want you to do your fuckin' job."

"Yeah," another voice broke in, "we don't wanna just fizzle away and end up to be somebody's tax write-off. We've all seen it happen to other bands and we don't want it to happen to us."

"And you want me to have all this arranged before you leave for South America?"

"Nope. What we want is a ... a ..."

"Letter of intent." Britain again.

"Yeah, a letter of intent that says that by a certain date you'll have all this crap set up or our contract with you will be null and void. Our lawyer will send you the letter to sign. If you don't, we don't go to South America, and we see you in court. Period. C'mon, you guys, let's go."

They marched out single file. They were giggling as they went and making comments about "the look on Blubberlips' face" and how "he was shitting bricks."

The secretary, whose name—Brenda—was printed on a small placard on her desk, smiled at them as they left and curled her upper lip into a snarl as the door closed. She started to type a letter.

"Uh, Brenda," I said, "you wanna tell Blubberlips that I'm here?"

She looked up, surprised.

"Oh, I'm sorry, Mr. ... Mr. ..."

"Hornblower. Leonard Hornblower."

"I'll tell him right now, Mr. Hornblower."

She picked up the phone, announced me, and listened to his answer.

"He says to go right in, Mr. ... um ..."

"Thank you, Bernice."

I walked down the narrow corridor and pushed open the door. There were two windows behind his desk. One gave a view of Fifty-eighth Street. The other framed a six-by-four section of concrete belonging to the building next door. The desk was one of those modern affairs made out of three strips of Formicaed wood, no drawers. The walls were covered with pictures of what I assumed were his clients.

"Sit down," he said, scowling from behind his desk.

"Just fine. And you?"

"Look, buster, I'm not in the mood for wisecracks. Say your piece and get out."

"Um, I was under the impression that you had a piece to say to me. You told me last night that you were going to think over what we talked about."

"Oh, yeah. You wanna make a deal. What's the matter? Nicky giving you a hotfoot?"

"Actually, if you examined the lump on his head, I think you'd find that he's been getting, not giving."

"Yeah?"

"Yeah. He, Jook, and Walt paid me a visit yesterday and they all ended up unconscious."

He chewed on that for a moment.

"All we're interested in is getting back what's ours. Once we do, you can relax, okay?"

"No. Not okay. As long as you think I know where it is, I feel more or less relaxed. I think that if and when you get it back, you'll get the bright idea that I know too much and then you'll take steps to uneducate me."

"So, what do you suggest?"

"I think the way we left it was for you to make a suggestion."

"Okay. All right. We don't tell the cops that you took

care of Blinky. How's that?"

"Well, if I had taken care of Blinky, I suppose that would be attractive. Only thing is—I didn't."

"Who did?"

"I was kinda thinkin' it was one of the guys on your team."

"That wouldn't make much sense, would it?"

"No, it wouldn't. On the other hand, I would venture to say that your boys are not over blessed with brains."

"And you are?"

"I got enough to not leave my goddamn wallet next to the body and then wait around for ten or fifteen people to see me leaning over him."

"Let's leave it at that, then. I don't care who did it. That creepy kid was a pain anyway. The point is the coke. I want it back."

"How much?"

"You mean, how much will I pay to get it?"

"No. I mean, how much do you want back?"

"What're you talkin' about?"

"When the boys paid me a visit yesterday, Nicky said he was twice as upset as when he'd heard there were three pounds gone. I assumed he meant that six more ..."

"What?" His face vibrated with the bellow.

"Nicky has assumed all along that I have the stuff or know where it is. Unfortunately, I don't. But I've told you that before and you didn't believe me. I say to myself, 'Self, if I don't have it or know where it is and Nicky keeps insisting I do, I begin to wonder if he doth protest too much.' Y'know what I mean? And now he's crying about six more pounds that even you don't know is missing. That stumps me. What does it do for you?"

He sucked in his bottom lip, chewed on it, and stared

at me. I'd taken the chance that Nicky hadn't told him about our fight or the news about more missing cocaine and it looked like I was right. He blinked his eyes back into focus and picked up the phone.

"Brenda, get Todd Eller at Butterfly Records in London. Tell him there's an emergency with The Hairdos and I gotta talk to him right away. Then call Nutty Nicky's and get Nicky on the line, and if they give you any bullshit about him not being there, tell whoever you talk to to tell Nicky that Hornblower's in my office trying to make a deal. Y'got that …? No, the name is Hornblower."

He hung up, drummed his fingers on the desk blotter and went back to staring at me. I figured we were waiting for a return call, so I shut up and stared back. His was not a pleasant face to stare at. I wished I had brought the *Times* with me so I could do the crossword puzzle instead. I got up and walked around his office looking at the pictures.

The phone rang.

"Yeah?" he said. "How's the connection …? Okay, put him through…. Hello, Todd? How ya doin' …? Listen, we got a little problem with The Hairdos…." He laughed. "No, no. Nothing like that. Remember I told you that it was just a matter of time before they got a fly up their ass about the contract and the debt and all that shit …? Well, they just came here hot from some lawyer who's given them some big ideas…. Yeah…. They want a new contract with me and a look at the books and royalty statements—the whole schmear…. That's what I told them, only they threatened to cancel the tour if I didn't sign a letter of intent that their lawyer's gonna draw up…. Right…. So what I'd like you to do is call your lawyers in New York and have them make copies of that rider we made the band sign when they signed with Butterfly … you know, that amendment that I wrote in afterward that says if they refuse to tour to support their album, you can hold in escrow any and all monies due them…. I know it's bullshit, but if we serve them with it, they'll have to jump into court and counter-sue, and we won't have to pay them the grand a month, and they'll fuckin' starve because we'll get the court to stop them from performing until the case is settled, and by that time they'll be washed up…. Yeah, I'm glad I made them sign it too. Those idiots didn't even read it. Every damn band I've ever handled gets to the point where they want me to put the earth, moon, and stars in their vest pocket for them…. I know. They're dumb assholes. Listen, as far as I'm concerned, I never met a rock musician who wasn't a dumb asshole…. Right…. Have your lawyer call me when he's ready to spring it…. Okay. Bye."

It was neatly done. I had thought, from what I'd heard, that The Hairdos had put him in a corner. I'd begun to think that maybe he wasn't so smart after all. Only it turned out that he'd expected them to pull their little *coup d'état* and had already prepared for it. They were now in the position of doing the tour or not being able to work at all. They were in the corner only they didn't know it yet.

He hunched over his desk and made a note in a black, spiral book. The phone buzzed. I sat down again.

"Yeah …? Yeah, put him through." He sat back, relaxed. "Hi, Nick. I … yeah, he's sitting right in front of me…. He wants to make a deal…. No, we haven't discussed a price…. Nicky, I think you should come up here right away…. I don't give a flying shit if it's a busy-type day at the store. Get your ass up here…. No. Not later—now…. Why? Is there some reason you don't want to see me …? Then be here inside a half-hour."

He hung up, sucked his lip again, and picked up the phone.

"Brenda, tell everybody to take the rest of the day off. When Nicky comes, show him in and then you go home too. Y'got that? I want everybody out by the time Nicky gets here."

He dropped the phone back on its cradle and grinned. It was the first smile I'd seen on his face. It raised the bags under his eyes, creased his cheeks, and thinned his lips. The guy looked smug. He'd just checkmated The Hairdos and figured me and Nicky were next. I had one trump left, but I wasn't going to play it unless I had to. We sat and looked across the desk at one another for fifteen or twenty minutes. I thought about Lisa. I thought about six pounds of cocaine c/o General Delivery. I thought about getting the hell out of that crummy office.

"What if," I said, "What if I don't want to be in the same room as Nicky? That man owes me one. If he was stupid enough to bump Blinky, he's stupid enough to bump me. And if he brings Walt, there's no way I'm gonna stay. I like my balls the way they are."

"Don't you worry. This is going to be a business meeting held in a businesslike manner."

"And how're you going to keep it that way?"

"Let me put it to you this way: Nicky is my dog. If I say heel, he heels."

"What about Walt?"

"Walt is Nicky's dog."

"Well, I'd really like to join your kennel, but I think I'm gonna blow this place. I don't mind being alone with you. In fact, it's a real learning experience. But two or three against one ain't my idea of fun. I tried it yesterday."

I started to stand.

"Hornblower, I told you that you were playing out of your league. You aren't going anywhere."

I don't know where he got it from. His hand never went to a pocket and there were no drawers in the desk and the one cabinet in the room was out of reach. But there it was, the third gun in as many days staring me back into my seat. I wasn't getting used to it. It looked like a .38, maybe a Bowdoin. It had a silencer.

"Do you think," I said, trying to keep my voice out of soprano range, "that I think that you'd shoot me here, in your own office?"

"Hey," he said, sitting up straight for the first time. It seemed guns did for his posture what knives did for Blinky's twitch. "If the police have found the body, then they've found your wallet, which means you're already a wanted man. I can give any number of reasons for shooting you and there's no one to say I'm wrong. Brenda won't even hear the shot."

"Yeah, but …"

"But what?"

I remembered how I had felt after Nicky had fired at me and it froze my tongue. I had to swallow a couple of times to thaw it out.

"But if you shoot me, you'll have done the same thing your dogs did to Blinky. I mean, you won't know about the coke."

"I'm glad you brought that up, prick. I think we should settle that once and …"

He picked up the buzzing phone.

"Yeah? Good. Send them in and go home."

Ten seconds passed and Nicky and Walt came in. They didn't notice the gun at first. They kept their eyes on me. Walt spoke first. His stupid cap was perched at a particularly stupid angle because of the wad of gauze taped to his head.

"Well, well, well. A reunion of sorts. You know, friend Leonard, I have not ceased thinking about you all day. I fervently hoped that the fates would deign to bring us together again, but I hardly thought it would be so soon"—he looked at Birmingham's gun—"and under such auspicious circumstances too."

Nicky spoke.

"Listen, Peter, why don't you just give him to me and Walt and we'll take him someplace and beat the goddamn truth out of him."

"Walt," said Birmingham, "stand over there, okay?" He motioned to the corner opposite the door, the farthest point from his desk.

"Nicky, exactly what are you going to beat out of him?"

Nicky looked from him to me and back again. He was nervously twirling his skinny tie around a finger.

"What d'ya mean? About the coke. What else?"

"That's what I mean. What else?"

"I don't follow you."

"If I said to you, 'Get the six pounds I gave to you last week and bring it here in an hour,' what would you say?"

"Why would you want me to bring it here?"

"Answer the question, prick."

"Aw, Peter, c'mon. Let's concentrate on Hornblower."

"Then he wasn't lying. It's gone, isn't it? You stupid fucking asshole. That means you're into me for nine pounds. That's a fuck of a lot of money, man. You owe me your life, and I just might take it."

"Okay, okay. It's gone. I don't know who took it, and I sure as hell don't know how. But I'm sure of one thing: that jerkoff knows about it."

"Maybe he does, and maybe he doesn't. Nicky, you're falling apart. Blinky takes three pounds from you easy as pie; you can't find Blinky; when you do find him, he's dead; you go out with two guys to get Hornblower and you all end up with lumps on your heads; then six more pounds turn up missing and you don't tell me about it. I wonder how much else you haven't told me. I wonder how much I need someone like you."

"What're you hassling me for?" Nicky was yelling. Scared yelling. "Hassle Hornblower. He's the guy with the answers."

"I wonder," Birmingham said, slowly turning the gun from me to Nicky. "Where did you hide the six pounds?"

Nicky started to speak, then stopped. He sat down in a chair by the door. He looked like he'd just swallowed some Drano.

"Where'd you hide it?"

"You don't think I ..."

"At this point, I'm the only one I trust. Things have been going wrong with you a little too consistently lately, Nick. I don't like it." He said it thoughtfully. "I don't like it at all."

Nicky looked at Walt, then at me, and back to Birmingham. He took a breath and stood.

"I don't have to listen to this shit. If the coke is gone, fuck it. It's no skin off my teeth. I didn't pay for it. If you think I still got it, you can go take a flying-type fuck for all I care."

He took a step toward the door.

"Hold it, Nicky," said Birmingham. "Get back in here, goddammit."

He shook the gun at Nicky as he spoke, like a schoolmarm does with her finger. The gun went off.

What happened next happened fast. I mean, boom, bam, boom, and finished. The bullet hit Nicky smack on the spinal cord, smashing his head against the door. Birmingham looked so shocked I thought he was going to swallow his tongue. Walt let out a roar and leaped at Birmingham like a middle linebacker breaking up a screen. Birmingham plugged him but Walt's momentum kept him going and he smacked into ole Blubberlips, tumbling him off the chair onto the floor. Once Walt stopped moving, he stopped moving—I mean for good. I got out the .45 and headed for the door. Birmingham wriggled out from under Walt and shot at me as he got up. He missed. I panicked and shot at his leg, only I forgot to hold my wrist, so the fucking recoil threw the bullet up just below his heart. The force of the slug pitched his body back just like some stuntman who gets shot in a Charles Bronson movie. He went through the window that looked out on the concrete slab and bounced back into the room.

20

I stood hunched over with one hand on the doorknob, the other outstretched, holding the gun. I couldn't move. I was trying to take in what just happened. My face felt hot and tense. I realized that I was holding my breath. I let it out, leaned against the wall, and sank to a crouch, my forearms draped over my knees. I let go of the gun. It dropped on my right foot. I sat there for a few minutes and tried to connect some thoughts together. All I could think of was that the smell of gun smoke reminded me of the cap guns I played with when I was small.

The phone rang four times. I remember thinking that dead men don't answer phones. It dawned on me that I was alone in a room with three dead men. Then I realized that I didn't know if they were dead.

Nicky was the closest. He was lying on his side, his legs folded behind him, cheek pressed against the door as if he were eavesdropping. There wasn't much blood. I put my finger on the big vein in the side of his neck. No pulse.

I moved to Walt. He was lying on his stomach. A thick leg was wrapped around the base of Birmingham's swivel chair. There was a small hole in his back; the bullet had gone clean through. Droplets of blood hung from the corner of his mouth and then oozed down his cheek like inchworms. No pulse.

Birmingham was spreadeagled on the carpet. The side of his leathery face that faced upward had already turned bluish-white, drained. I had to lift him slightly to get my finger on his neck. A pool of blood had formed under him. It made me shiver and drop him. There was a sickening, squishy sound as his weight pressed the thick liquid into the carpet. No pulse.

"Three dead men. Three dead men. See how they run. See how they run."

I softly sang it over and over as I moved around the room. I wiped the .45 with a handkerchief and put it in Nicky's right hand. I wiped the arm of the chair and was about to wipe the doorknob when I realized that having no fingerprints on it was a bad idea. I lifted Nicky's left arm and wrapped his hand around the inside knob. That wasn't so smart either, because I still had to get out. I opened the door about a foot, slipped through, and lifted his arm again. It was a bitch getting his hand to cover the knob from the other side, but I did it and let the weight of his body shut the door.

I took similar precautions with the orange vinyl couch and the outer door. I pressed the elevator button with my elbow and ran down nine flights so the elevator man wouldn't see me as I came through the stairway door into the lobby.

I walked to Lexington and Fifty-ninth and got on the subway. A local took me to Twenty-third and Park. I walked from there to the hotel. I can't remember anything in particular from the time I left the office till I got to our room on the sixth floor, except I noticed again what a spectacularly beautiful day it was. I had certainly made use of it. I had done something. The only question was if I'd done it well.

Lisa was sitting on the bed, propped up against the wall, writing in a small notebook. She glanced at me as I came in.

"Whose ghost did you see?" she said, smiling. "You look terrible."

I sat in the chair by the window, looked down on Lexington Avenue, and tapped my foot.

"Earth to Lenny. Come in, please."

I got up, walked into the bathroom, and threw up.

"Are you okay? What's the matter?"

My eyes stung and my chest and stomach ached. I rinsed my face with cold water and walked back to the chair.

"Something bad happened uptown, right?" she said, bending over me, trying to make me meet her gaze.

"Yeah, you could say that. I don't know, maybe it was good. I don't know."

"Well, what the hell happened?"

I looked at her and tried to decide if it would serve any purpose to tell her. If I did tell her, it would make her an accessory to whatever the cops charged me with. I had little doubt that they would charge me. Brenda, the secretary, would finger me even if my lame attempts to wipe away the fingerprints worked.

"Lenny, wake up. What happened?"

Accessory? Who was I trying to kid?

"I just left an office in a building on Fifty-eighth Street."

"Yes."

"I went there to try to make a deal with the guy who bosses around the guys we tangled with yesterday."

"Go on."

"I didn't really go there to make a deal. I was just trying to divide him from his dogs."

"Dogs?"

"An enemy divided is almost an ally."

"Did you fall on your head or something?"

"So I went there and he called his dogs and they came up and everybody else went home."

"I don't know what you're talking about."

"I played all my trump cards. I mean, I couldn't believe it. It was working. If the asshole had thought about it, he would have realized that Nicky …"

"Nicky?"

"… couldn't have ripped off the coke. But Nicky hadn't told him it was gone, so he just jumped to conclusions."

"Do you want a drink?"

"Then Nicky started to leave and he shot him. Not on purpose—I don't think it was on purpose."

"Shot him? Shot who? Who shot who?"

"Then Walt got shot and he shot at me and I shot at him."

She ran to the phone, called room service, and ordered a bottle of whisky.

"And now they're all dead. Holy shit. I've never seen anything like it."

I guess I was in shock, if being in shock means nonstop, monotonal conversation. Lisa kept trying to talk to me, to get me to explain what I was saying, but I just kept droning on for I don't know how long.

The whisky came and I started drinking between sentences. I talked about the post office, the warehouse, a brown van, speaker cabinets, Snappy Comebacks, Hofstra U., interesting-type things, stupid caps, Hershey Kisses, nipples, unmade beds, Roxanne. By the time I got around to .45-caliber automatics, I'd downed nearly half a quart of whisky. I took a breath after a swallow, put the bottle on the floor, and shut up.

Lisa had been making the fake smile, clown sounds that healthy people make when they're faced with the permanently demented. After I quieted down, she began to make conversation in the hope, I suppose, of rousing me from catatonia.

"I went to my apartment while you were gone. José wasn't there so I couldn't ask him what you wanted to know. I got Blinky's address book like you wanted."

I stood up quickly, which was a mistake. The force of the booze hit me hard and I fell forward onto the bed. Lisa lifted my feet onto the covers and turned me over on my back.

I began to feel the pleasant glow of drunkenness. I sat up and started to put some thoughts in order.

What happened at Birmingham's office was clearly self-defense, although trying to cover up my presence there was just as clearly criminal. I hadn't had any choice though. Already suspected of one murder, to have it known that I was alone in a room with three bullet-riddled corpses would not help at all.

"Lenny, please, tell me what happened."

I looked at her and laughed.

"I think I already did."

"You said someone shot someone. Who?"

"I was in a room with three guys: Nicky, Walt, and a man named Birmingham. Birmingham shot Nicky in the head accidentally. Then he shot Walt not so accidentally. Then he shot at me and missed. I shot him. They're all dead."

"I don't understand."

"What's to understand? Dead is dead."

"But why? I don't see any connections."

I was good and bombed by that time and I didn't care anymore that I didn't trust her. I told her everything—everything from that first phone call to our present conversation, except the part about the six pounds of coke in the post office and how it got there. I made no judgments, no inferences, just the facts, ma'am, just the facts. I'm pretty good at that kind of reporting. I can remember most conversations verbatim and I don't mix up the sequence of events. It's something you learn when you deal with divorce lawyers.

When I finished—it took the better part of an hour—she took my hand and kissed the center of the palm.

"Thank you," she said.

"Thank you? Thank you for what?"

"Never mind. What do we do now?"

"We gotta catch the guy who rips pins out of dead punks' noses."

"How?"

"We're gonna go fishin'. We're gonna bait a hook and see who bites. Where's that address book?"

I had reached that stage of intoxication where my

mind works clearly but the liquor adds melodrama to the words I choose. I didn't have any particular plan in mind. Blinky was killed for a reason. I could think of three or four, but none that fit all the facts. I had to throw some gas on the fire and see who got burned.

I had her call Nutty Nicky's and leave a message for Stu and Jook. She said she was Birmingham's secretary and that Nicky wanted them to meet him at ten P.M. at AC-DC's. Then she called AC-DC's and left the same message for Artie Salt.

It was five o'clock. My drunken lucidity gave way to grogginess. I asked Lisa to wake me at eight.

I fell into a kind of half-sleep. A dream of grins and blood dissolved into the bureau against the wall. I realized I was awake and turned over to face the window. Thoughts of jail and courtrooms and police melted into visions of Lisa grinning evilly, holding her small pistol, pointing it at me. It went off. I woke up, opened my eyes, and realized a truck had backfired. I turned onto my stomach and clutched the pillow to my cheek. I was at AC-DC's with an axe, chopping away at the bar. A pair of turquoise cowboy boots stood next to me. I put them on and fell down. I couldn't get up. My face was lying in a pool of liquor. I woke up and found I'd drooled whisky-flavored spittle onto the pillow. I turned the pillow over and curled up on my side. I was sweating. I imagined I could feel the alcohol seep through my pores. The dream I'd had of Lisa in the black bodysuit recurred complete with her balancing act on the pink elephant. This time she stepped off and started pushing me, a blank look on her face. I woke up and looked up at her. She was shaking my shoulder and wiping my brow with a cool, damp cloth.

"You were moaning in your sleep. I think you have

a fever."

"No," I said, slowly sitting up. "I'm a middle-aged man who had too much to drink."

"It's eight. What now?"

"I'm going to take a shower and then we're going to get some dinner and then go to that goddamn club."

The shower, as usual, relaxed me and I stayed too long. I hoped the bodies on Fifty-eighth Street would stay undiscovered until the following morning. At this point, everything indirectly depended on the live cruds not knowing about the dead cruds.

I came out of the bathroom to find Lisa doing exercises on the carpet. The effects of the booze had pretty much worn off, although I still felt a little light-headed.

"When's the Olympics?"

"Don't joke. If you got some exercise once in a while, you wouldn't be so porky."

"Thanks, but no thanks."

She changed her clothes and put on some makeup. We went to a café or bistro or whatever on Third Avenue. I had roast chicken and rice. She ordered breast of capon in cream sauce.

"What time are we going to the club?" she asked.

"You're not going."

"Why not?"

"'Cause I said so."

"Fuck you."

"Okay."

"Why not? What the hell am I going to do?"

"I want you to go back to your apartment and wait for me to call."

"No phone."

"Shit. I forgot about that. Go to that Latin Chinese Palace or whatever the hell they call it."

"It's The Latin Mandarin. Why am I doing that?"

"You have to be someplace I can reach you in case I blow this thing. I may just call you and have you call the cops if something goes wrong with this little scam."

"What is this little scam, anyway?"

"Don't worry about it. Just do what I say."

"We're back to that, I see."

"What?"

"Keeping me in the dark 'cause you don't trust me."

"I'm very possibly trusting you with my life. Is that okay?"

"Christ. You're impossible."

"Yeah."

It was nine-thirty or so when I got to the club. There weren't many people hanging around outside except for the usual complement of winos. The night was clear and warm. A slight breeze snaked along the Bowery, bringing newspaper shreds in its wake.

I pushed the creaky wooden door and saw Dora at her post behind the small table. She looked at me, took a moment to recognize my face, and then looked surprised.

"You better get out of here," she said, low-toned. "Nicky and Birmingham are going to be here soon."

"Yeah? Who told you that?"

"I know more about what goes on in this place than anyone, and I'm telling you that those turds are going to be here at ten, and it's nearly that now."

"I'll take my chances. Is Artie here?"

"Yeah. He's downstairs."

"What about Stu and Jook?"

"They haven't shown up." She knit her brow and tilted her head. "Hey, aren't the cops after you?"

I walked by her without paying the cover charge.

She didn't say anything.

It was about as crowded as the first night I'd been there, maybe fifty people, all leaning. A poster on the door said: "AUDITION NIGHT." I wondered if they ever had Punk comedians.

Tory was sitting on the bench opposite the bar rummaging about in her big canvas bag. She looked up and didn't, or wouldn't, recognize me. I was glad she didn't. She couldn't have been more than twenty-two or so, and the memory of our little encounter embarrassed me.

Guys on the stage were moving equipment around. What a crummy job. I wondered where those guys came from. They all looked and dressed kind of alike. I stood at the bar and ordered a Scotch. I figured the cruds would congregate at the same table as last time, so I moved into the shadows behind the cigarette machine, where I could get a clear view of them and where they probably wouldn't notice me.

A couple of Punks walked by. I really hadn't seen all that many of them, and this was the fourth time I'd been to the club. Most of the kids were the same scruffy, blue-jeaned types you see on the streets. There was a small group of guys that dressed like Nicky: tight black pants, black, three-button jackets with narrow lapels, small-collared, white cotton shirts, skinny-as-hell ties, and sneakers or pointy black shoes. They all looked like Rod Serling.

Stu and Jook came in, nodded to Dora, and went straight to the table. A nice red welt spread out over the rim of Jook's sunglasses. Artie lumbered into view from the passageway next to the stage. He joined them. Stu started talking and making nervous gestures. Jook said something that shut Stu up. Artie looked bored.

I made my way to the table.

"Hi, guys," I said. "What's shakin'?"

Stu swiveled in his seat, looked up at me, and mumbled, "Oh, shit."

Jook half-rose, thought the better of it, and contented himself with a snarl.

Artie told me, "Lose yourself, creep."

"I got a message from Nicky and Birmingham."

They all did the same double take in unison. Artie spoke first.

"What's that supposed to mean?"

"I don't know how to say it any clearer. Nicky and Birmingham gave me a message to give to you."

"I don't trust this guy, y'know?" Jook said to Artie. "Why would Nick give him a goddamn message for us?"

"Hey," I said, "it doesn't matter to me. I'd just as soon not look at any of you for the rest of my life. They got me in a corner, so I gotta do what they say. I sort of work for Birmingham now, you might say."

"Doin' what?" Artie sat back and looked at me.

"Well, for one thing, delivering messages."

I noticed that Dora had sat at the next table with her back to us.

"Okay," said Artie, "spill. What is it?"

"He said the cops have a line on who killed Blinky. He wants whoever has the gun to bring it to his office by midnight so plans can be made to get rid of it and get the coke back."

The second I said it I knew it was too strong. I moved to my left a bit to get a clear view of their faces. Stu gulped, reddened, and looked like his eyes were going to pop. Jook screwed his face into a mass of sarcasm. Artie didn't change expression.

"Last I heard," said Artie, "the only guy the cops

had a line on was you."

"Yeah, well, if that was the last you heard, you're behind the times. I'm just telling you what Nicky and Birmingham told me to tell you."

"You're full of shit, you know that?" Jook said as he lit a cigarette and flicked the match at me.

"Where are they now?" asked Artie.

"I don't know," I said. "I spoke to them on the phone."

"Nicky told me that he and Walt were going to Birmingham's to straighten something out," said Stu. "Maybe Hornblower's on the level."

"Straighten out what?" Artie asked.

"He didn't say."

"Well, you guys bat it around. I delivered my message. I'm out of it now."

I turned and walked toward the door. It was nearly ten-thirty. Dora passed me, heading for her table. She didn't say anything. She had to have heard everything from where she'd been sitting.

I crossed the Bowery and sat in a doorway facing the club. I was going to wait until midnight for one or all of them to head to Birmingham's. I was going to follow and then call the cops to find them there with three corpses and maybe the gun that killed Blinky. It was a long shot. My bait hadn't been very tasty. If it didn't work, if none of them went for it, I'd have to turn myself in the next day and talk fast. There were too many things pointing at me—no real proof, but certainly enough to indict me. I could yak about hijacking and drugs and maybe toss some suspicion in another direction, but somehow it all came zooming back at me.

Around eleven-fifteen Stu and Jook came out. They hung around the doorway, talking. At one point Jook grabbed Stu by the collar and brought him nose to nose. Then he let go and they walked inside.

I got to thinking about when my grandmother had died. A few days before she kicked, she'd asked to see me. Her insides were bloated with inoperable cancer. She had a lot of trouble just talking. She told me she'd had a dream where a nurse had come in and slapped her hands, saying that Grandma had been a very bad girl. Then the hospital had caught fire and everything around her started crackling. She used "crackling" in nearly every sentence like it had some special meaning. Anyway, everything and everybody were burning and crackling, and the nurse who'd slapped her had turned into a "nice young man" who told her that she'd died and now she was in hell. She screamed and crackled and tried to ask what it was she'd done that put her in hell. The nice young man smiled and crackled and told her that he wasn't allowed to say. All he could tell her was that she deserved it and knowing that should make her feel better. She went into a coma right after telling me her dream.

I thought about how I could go to jail very easily if nothing worked out that night. I'd been drawn into this situation without ever once having any control over it. There wasn't even a nice young man to tell me I deserved it. Things were crackling.

Midnight came and went and none of the cruds had left. I sighed, went to a phone booth, and called information to get the number of The Latin Mandarin. Lisa sounded tired when she got on the phone.

We helloed.

"Well?" she said.

"Well, nothing. It's all over. I give up. I'm going to turn myself in tomorrow and hope for the best. Maybe they'll give me my wallet back."

"But ..."

"But nothing. Listen, I'll meet you at your place in a half-hour, okay?"

"Okay. Bring a bottle of wine or something."

"Good idea."

I went into a liquor store and bought some Scotch and some wine. I started to hail a cab and realized I didn't have enough money left, so I walked to Seventh Avenue and took a train to Seventy-ninth and Broadway.

I don't often get depressed. I'm usually a firm believer in the what-goes-down-must-come-up-again state of things, but, walking from the subway station to Lisa's, I felt like shit: a third-rate nobody who'd gotten in over his head.

José wasn't at the door. He was probably home nursing a bruised head like everybody else in this damned case. I walked into the apartment. The lock was still broken. Lisa was in the kitchen. She'd straightened the place up as well as she could. The busted sofa was piled in the corner near the bay window. The stuffing from the cushions had been swept up, the various drawers and cabinets put back in order.

I sat on the carpet by the undamaged glass coffee table. It looked out of place amid the chaos. The porcelain elephants that supported it sneered at me. Lisa heard the clinking of bottles as I took them out of the bag.

"Is that you?" she called.

"No."

She stepped into the living room with two glasses and sat down beside me. She kissed my cheek and spoke.

"Are you really going to turn yourself in?"

"There's nothing else for me to do. They'd catch me

sooner or later, and it'd be worse for me then."

"What will happen?"

"Well"—I poured six fingers of Scotch into my glass and filled hers with wine—"they'll book me right away for murder. Then they'll grill the hell out of me. I'll either be denied bail or it'll be far too high for me to raise."

I waited for some kind of reaction. I didn't get one.

"Then I'll tell them a story about Blinky and my involvement with him without mentioning your name, 'cause that'd make you a liar. I'll just say he stole my wallet, which is true, and then say I didn't see him again after he ripped it off, which is bullshit. They'll ask where I've been for the last few days and I'll bullshit some more. If by some miracle they haven't tied me to Birmingham, Nicky, and Walt, I'll have to shut up about the drugs and the hijacking. If they have tied me to them, I'll have to come clean, and that'll open a can of worms that … shit, I don't even want to think about it. Let's get drunk."

She eyed me for a couple of seconds and sighed. "Lenny, I lied to you about something."

"What was that?"

"About what I told you about Blinky inheriting money from his father—it's not true. I only said it because I was angry with you for suspecting me, and I wanted to tell you something that would … I don't know. I wanted to get back at you."

I laughed and shook my head as I rearranged my feet under me. My shoe bumped against the pink elephant, sounding a clear note.

"That was one of the things I believed. Can you beat that? Y'know, I still think that …"

A loud, loud click went off in my head. My face must have shown it.

"Lenny, what's wrong?" she said. "What's wrong?"

"You got a hammer?"

"A hammer?"

"I didn't ask for an echo." My voice was harsh, harsher than it'd been in a long time. "Get me a goddamn hammer."

"What for?"

"When I was here that time when I slugged Blinky and you were in the kitchen washing dishes, I ... just get me a hammer."

"Okay, okay."

She went to the kitchen and returned with a claw hammer. I lifted the glass top off the elephants' backs. Using the wine bottle, I tapped the pink one and then the white one. The pink gave a nice tinkly chime. The white's was as dull as when I'd kicked it three days before. I raised the hammer above the white one.

"You want to tell me anything before I smash this thing to bits?" I asked. I hadn't used that tone of voice since the last time I beat up Roxanne.

She opened her mouth, closed it, inhaled, exhaled, and wiped her hands on an imaginary apron.

"Well?"

"She knows," said Dora.

She was standing in the doorway. Lisa looked at her and gagged. Dora all by herself isn't enough to make you gag. But Dora aiming a small-caliber pistol, a familiar small-caliber pistol, at your head—that could make you blow some chunks.

21

"Put down the hammer, please."

Dora's voice was as dull and lifeless as ever. She

closed the door behind her and took a couple of steps toward us.

"Don't try anything," she said. "I've already used this gun once and it wasn't hard. I could do it again." She was relaxed, even bored.

"Listen, bitch lady," she said to Lisa, "I've come for it—all of it. I was willing to share. You could have had half."

Lisa set her jaw. She was getting mad. Dora went on.

"You almost had me going for a while. All that talk about a fall guy. You've been with him for days and here he is still walking around."

"You stupid little fool," Lisa said. "You idiot." She packed a lot of loathing into those two words. "Everything is …"

"Shut up, dammit." A little anger crept into Dora's monotone.

I cleared my throat, not to get attention. I suddenly had difficulty breathing. Dora looked at me.

"You sure got taken for a ride. It wasn't supposed to end like this though. That goddamn blackout screwed it all up. It gave Artie time to move the body. She dropped your wallet there, you know." She glanced at Lisa. "That was her bright idea."

"Lenny, don't believe her. I don't know what she's talking about."

Dora laughed without amusement.

"She's good, isn't she? She fooled the hell out of Blinky. She filled him full of coke and sent him down there that night. She made him take the gun and told him to kill Birmingham and Nicky. Is that hysterical or what?"

Lisa's mouth was shut tight. I could see her jaw muscles working.

"She figured they'd blow Blinky away and then have the coke all to herself. You were a loose end. You didn't quit when she told you to. That's why the wallet had to be left there. But she didn't think about me. I told Blinky when to steal the coke and how. Me and Blinky were going to split the profits and then I was going to leave this fucking town. I wasn't ever going to work in that fucking dive again. But then she horned in."

Her voice was getting high and squeaky. Her body was tense and her gun hand shook. It was aimed at Lisa.

"Nobody knows what it's like working at a place like that night after night, seeing the same deadheads parade in and out of there. It saps you. You feel like you're a part of the Bowery, a part of the filth." She laughed. "Can you even imagine that?"

"Now listen, honey," said Lisa, sounding like an Eighth Avenue hooker, "put that thing down and let's come to some kind of agreement."

"No. Uh-uh. Forget it, honey." She mimicked Lisa. "You're gonna shoot Galahad and then you're gonna commit suicide. I've gone through hell for this dope, and I mean to get it all with no loose strings."

"You're crazy. You're crazy."

"I'm crazy? Hah," she said. Then she spoke to me. "She says I'm crazy. You know how she found out about the coke?"

I shook my head.

"She balled Blinky and got him to talk. She's good at it, y'know, getting men to talk. But I don't have to tell you that, do I?"

She looked and sounded like she was going to crack up. She seemed to enjoy the talking so I prompted her. "But why did you shoot Blinky?"

"Why?" She glanced at the ceiling as if that was the

stupidest question she'd ever heard. "Because of you, that's why. I called Lady Bitch here right after I spoke to you at Beefy's. She told me you were the fall guy. After Nicky and them had taken care of Blinky, I was supposed to drop the wallet nearby for the police to find, except I didn't have the wallet, she did. She was supposed to bring it and leave right away, but you saw her and rushed her outside before she had a chance to give it to me.

"I went back to the alley and met Blinky. He was coming down from the coke and falling apart. He didn't want to fight those guys. He didn't have the nerve. He wanted to give it back. He handed me the gun and said he was through and he was going to get the coke and return it. I didn't even think twice; I was so fucking pissed at him. Even when he was lying there, I was so mad I ripped that stupid pin out of his nose."

Lisa was calming down. Her face was set in a blank stare. I'd known all along that she'd been hiding something, stringing me along, but I hadn't thought it was something like that. I hadn't thought that at all. But then, I really hadn't wanted to think.

Dora continued. She giggled between sentences.

"But that goddamn blackout: Who could've known? It gave Artie time to move the body. No one even noticed or cared that it was there, what with all the confusion when the lights went out. I wanted it found at the club. I wanted a big scandal and all that shit about stealing equipment and everything to come out. God, I hate that place. And you," she said to me, "Bitch Lady had to keep you in sight and know what you were up to because the blackout delayed everything and she wanted to pick the right moment to call the cops." To Lisa: "Why didn't you turn him in? Everything was perfect. He would have told about

Birmingham and Nicky and we would have been home free."

Lisa kept staring at her. Dora stared back. Then Dora laughed.

"You mean … you mean that you … you and him were … I don't believe it." More laughing. "You fell for him? Him?" The laughter was getting out of control. "I've been sitting at home sweating and wondering what was going wrong and … I never thought of that, not once. My God. Some cold bitch you turned out to be. What a joke."

"Shut up," Lisa snarled.

"What about me?" Dora trembled in anger as she spoke. "What'd you think I was going to do? Did you think I was going to stand by and shut up while you ran off with Galahad to the South Seas? Brother, are you stupid. I followed him here from AC's. I heard the crap he handed to Artie and them. I knew you put him up to it just like you did Blinky."

She'd crossed over into hysteria. Her eyes were tearing; her body vibrated. It must have been quite a feat holding all that emotion locked behind those tired eyes. They weren't tired anymore. They were blazing.

"Get out of here." Lisa screamed. "Everything was set up. They'll be here any minute."

"Who?" I said, moving toward Lisa.

Dora was past listening, past talking. She raised the gun awkwardly and aimed at my head.

"No, you idiot." Lisa yelled. "Not now. Not now."

She stepped toward Dora. The gun exploded. Lisa had moved in front of me and, I found out later from the papers, was struck under the right eye, which was fitting. Blinky's tic was under his right eye.

Dora was breathing hard through her mouth. Her lips were parted but her teeth were clenched, making her breathing sound like a fireplace forge.

"You were supposed to get it first," she said. "So now I'll have to make you be the suicide."

She walked toward me, her arm outstretched. You don't know what cold fear is till someone walks slowly toward you, pointing a gun at your face. I knew she wanted to get close enough to make powder burns, so I started moving backward at the same pace. I bumped into the wall. She brought the gun about a foot from my face. She held her breath. I closed my eyes.

Someone knocked on the door. She turned her head. I grabbed her wrist and bent her arm down. The gun fired. She went limp and slid down my body. Her lip caught on my belt buckle on the way down.

The door swung open. Three uniforms and one guy in a gray suit rushed in. I looked at Lisa sprawled on the carpet with two cops bending over her, shut my eyes, and cried for the first time in thirty-seven years.

22

That was about four months ago. Now it's November. The temperature dropped below freezing for the first time today. I took a long walk this morning. The sky and the city are gray and the air is damp-cold, my favorite weather. They released me yesterday and gave back my wallet.

Dora had been wrong. Lisa hadn't fallen for me, not by a long shot. That night had been the time she'd chosen for fingering me. When I'd called and told her that I was going to turn myself in the next day, she'd called the cops and invited them up to collar me. I don't think she'd wanted to do it that way, but my decision to turn myself in would've changed the cops' perspective too much. I don't have the slightest idea what story she was going to give them, but I'm sure it would have been airtight. She was good with stories.

The cops had handcuffed me and taken me to a precinct house uptown. I called a lawyer I'd once done some work for and he said he didn't handle criminal cases but offered to call Legal Aid.

I was shipped to Riker's Island and chained to about twenty guys in a kind of waiting room. I was the only white. The fellow next to me was in drag and a few of the others were arguing about who was going to "get her." I got thrown into a crowded cell, fell asleep, and woke up to find my pockets picked clean, which meant that I didn't even have a cigarette.

I was booked as a material witness and later for first-degree murder and about ten lesser charges.

My lawyer was a young guy named Finkel who had long brown hair and wore jeans and a brown corduroy jacket. I told him the whole story minus the six pounds and he told me to tell it to the assistant D.A. and sign a statement. He said if what I told him about the hijacking and the drugs was true, he could get a lot of the charges dropped.

They found the coke in the white elephant and the stolen equipment in the warehouse on Delancey Street. Stu, Jook, and Artie were picked up and questioned. Artie was released, then arrested later for being an accessory after the fact, because he moved the body, and released again for lack of evidence. Stu and Jook were indicted for grand theft and trafficking in narcotics. They were convicted on the first count and acquitted on the second, again for lack of evidence.

Finkel was pretty good. It turned out that there was no proof that I had been to Birmingham's office— Brenda couldn't remember my name or pick me out of a lineup—so he had that part of my statement expunged on some kind of technicality.

It was easy to prove that Dora had killed Lisa and that I had killed Dora in self-defense. The gun had stayed in her hand and the cops said I didn't have time to put it there because they had come in right after hearing the shot.

I still had a few felonies and misdemeanors against me, but Finkel told Assistant D.A. Morton that I would be more than willing to turn state's evidence against Stu and Jook. That, along with the fact that Morton liked me because he thought that my story was "preposterously funny" and that I was "monumentally stupid," was enough to convince him to drop the rest of the charges.

Finkel got me transferred to a minimum-security prison in Dutchess County while all this was going on, and that wasn't too bad. I got a lot of thinking done. Mostly I thought about six pounds of cocaine sitting in the post office on Thirty-fourth Street. If the papers were right about the street value of three pounds, it meant that my cache was worth about a half million dollars on the street. My dreams of a two-bedroom apartment changed to visions of a town house.

I'm going to the post office tomorrow.

23

I decided to wait a few months before I tried to get rid of the coke. I went back to driving a cab to pay the rent. I did that only because I knew it would be temporary.

I was worried about how I was going to get rid of

the stuff. I didn't know any dealers and I didn't know about price and weight. As it turned out, I shouldn't have worried at all.

I'd gotten the parcel out of the post office, brought it home, and put it on the kitchen table. I decided to hide the stuff behind the radiator next to the stove and resolved not to take it out till I was ready to sell it. I jammed it behind the pipes and didn't touch it until February.

A blizzard blew last night. The radio said it was the biggest in years. Today is my forty-eighth birthday. The streets are clogged with snow so there's no point in trying to drive the cab today. I'm sitting on the couch in the living room staring at six pounds of cocaine on the wooden table in front of me.

Mice have chewed holes through the plastic wrappers. They didn't do much damage. It doesn't look like they ate much of the coke. But something is very wrong. I guess maybe it was the heat from the radiator and air getting in through the holes in the plastic. The stuff is caked and greasy and moldy and yellowed. I think it's ruined.

I'm going to try and find a liquor store that's open, buy a bottle of Scotch, and get wall-eyed drunk. Tomorrow I'm going to go down to the *Voice* office and place an ad.

"ZZZ. Will do private work for a fee. Complete discretion."

THE END

John P. Browner lived in Greenwich Village during the 70's. An habitué of the downtown clubs that spawned the Punk/New Wave music scene, he wrote *Death of a Punk* in 1977-78. It was originally published by Pocket Books in 1980. Currently, he lives with his wife, the writer Lisa Yarger, and his daughter, Greta, in

Munich, Germany, where he owns and operates The Munich Readery, an English secondhand bookshop.

BLACK GAT BOOKS offers the best in reprint crime fiction from the 1950s-1970s. New titles appear every month, and each book is sized to 4.25" x 7", just like they used to be. Collect them all.

Stark House Press

1315 H Street, Eureka, CA 95501 (707) 498-3135
griffinskye3@sbcglobal.net www.starkhousepress.com
Available from your local bookstore or direct from the publisher

Made in the USA
Columbia, SC
03 November 2024

45552400R00120